The Halsey Brothers Series

Marshal in Petticoats
Outlaw in Petticoats
Miner in Petticoats
Doctor in Petticoats
Logger in Petticoats

OUTLAW IN PETTICOATS

The Halsey Brothers Series

by

Paty Jager

Windtree Press
Beaverton, Oregon

OUTLAW IN PETTICOATS

Publishing History
First Edition
Outlaw in Petticoats 2008 (Ebook & Print)

Second Edition
Outlaw in Petticoats 2011 (Ebook only)

Third Edition
Outlaw in Petticoats 2022 (Ebook & Print)

Published in the United States of America
ISBN 978-1-957638-27-0

Foreword

The town depicted in this story was an actual mining town on the John Day River in Oregon. At the time the story takes place, the town was called Susanville. But when the miners stole the post office (yes, they really did) thus taking the name of the town with them, Susanville became Galena after an ore found with silver.

If you travel to Galena, you will find a few buildings. And up the canyon at Susanville you can find remnants of a small community and the footings of a stamp mill.

Acknowledgements

Special thanks to my friend, mentor, and editor, Nicole, who believed in my storytelling and honed my writing.

To my mom, Regina Norman, who believed in me and told me I could do anything if I set my mind to it.

Chapter 1

Zeke Halsey patted the pocket on his vest. The tintype his new sister-in-law, Darcy, found while kidnapped by outlaws resided close to his heart. How the likeness of his parents ended up in a pile of loot in the outlaw's hideout had all the Halsey brothers perplexed.

He took the stairs of the boarding house in McEwen two at a time. He hadn't laid his eyes on Maeve Loman the pretty, prickly school marm since his youngest brother Gil showed up at the family mine with a woman dressed like a boy and her brother.

After witnessing his baby brother marry Darcy, Zeke was more determined than ever to get Maeve to come around to his thinking. He planned to start by showing her he came from good stock and put one more reason for her to reject his marriage proposal behind them.

Maeve met him at the door.

He stared taking in her perfection. Her black

hair glimmered like a raven's wing in the sunlight.

Her delicious pink lips, he hadn't sampled near enough, fluttered a moment before straightening into a firm line. She'd wanted to give him a welcoming smile and thought about it. That was the problem with Maeve, she thought too darn much.

"I brought something for you to see," he said, removing his hat and following her swaying backside into the parlor.

She sat primly on the wooden chair and gazed up at him. "What did you bring?"

He sat, placing his hat on his knee and reached for his vest pocket. Panic widened her dark blue eyes.

When he slipped the tintype out, relief relaxed her pretty features. She'd thought he was going to propose, again. He grinned. One of these days he was going to ask her to marry him, and she wouldn't be able to avoid answering.

"It's a tintype of my parents. We'd thought it was lost, but Darcy, the girl who married Gil, found it."

She took the tintype and stared at it before running her finger over the faces. Her brow furrowed, and she looked up at him. "These can't be your parents."

"Why can't they be my folks? Because they're too pretty?" Zeke watched her continue to stare at the tintype in her shaking hands. The lacy curtain in the window behind Maeve framed her form, giving her a fragile appearance.

"No. Pa said that man was his brother."

Zeke jerked his attention from Maeve's comely attributes back to her angular face and wide eyes.

He nearly choked from her contorted expression. Memories of all the times he'd stolen a kiss and been tempted to do more drifted in his thoughts. The idea they could be kin, and something else he couldn't place, didn't set well with her. He saw it in her troubled, blue eyes.

"That can't be." He bolted out of the sturdy, yet comfortable chair, he favored when visiting and crossed the room in two strides. Zeke stared down at the picture of his parents. "My pa didn't have any brothers, or sisters, for that matter. They all died on the way out west. Only him and an uncle survived the trip."

Her steely stare glimmered with unshed tears. "My pa had this tintype. It sat on our mantel. He'd look at it and tell stories of how he and his brother," she placed a finger gently on his father's likeness, "this man, played jokes."

The anguish and longing in her eyes said she wasn't making it up, but his head and heart knew she had to be.

"Come on." He grabbed her hand and roughly pulled her to her feet.

She jerked her hand from his and glared at him. Her odd habit of curling and uncurling her fingers right about holster height caught his attention. She only did that when she was annoyed or distraught.

"I'm sorry. I didn't mean to be so rough." He ran a hand down her slender arm. Nothing would ever make him hurt Maeve. He'd made up his mind the minute he set eyes on her; she'd be his no matter how long it took. "Let's go see my brothers. Ethan's old enough to remember if Pa had a brother I don't know about.

She stared at the hand still resting on her arm. "Do you think that is proper?"

"Escorting you? Why shouldn't it be?" He slid his hand to her elbow.

She gulped and veiled her eyes with thick, black lashes, "We could be cousins."

The realization they could be that closely related didn't set well with his plans. Damn! If she and he were— He put a finger under her chin, lifting her face to see whatever expression she'd allow. One thing he'd learned while courting her, she didn't let anyone see what she felt. This was the first time in a year she'd shown emotions without thinking it through first.

"We aren't related. We can't be. I wouldn't feel the desires I do if we were blood. That much I'm sure of."

She shook her head, looking away before he could glimpse what she thought.

"Come on, let's get this settled. I want to put your mind at rest." He pulled her to the door of the parlor. "Go to your room and get your shawl." He gave her a nudge toward the staircase leading to the second floor of the boarding house.

"You two going out?" asked Mrs. White, the widow, who rented rooms to the school teachers of McEwen. She stood in the kitchen doorway, wiping her hands on the white apron draped over her short, stout body.

"I'm taking Miss Loman to my brother's for the afternoon. Don't worry about fixing dinner for her. We'll feed her." Zeke retrieved his hat from the coat tree near the front door and waited for Maeve.

It didn't take that long to grab a shawl.

He moved to the stairs, resting his hand on the smooth, oak banister as she appeared at the top. His breath whooshed out. She still had on an everyday dress, but her curves were silhouetted by the long window on the landing. Lips the color of summer roses pursed in thought as she descended the stairs. The sadness in her eyes told him she already believed the worst. She rarely smiled. There were few moments since courting Maeve he'd seen unbridled happiness on her face. He wanted to be the person to give her a permanent smile.

Zeke held out a hand. Hesitantly, she took hold, and he led her out to his wagon full of supplies.

He grasped her about the waist to lift her onto the wagon. She twisted her neck to look at him. It took all his control to keep from brushing his lips to hers. He knew from the stiffening of her body and the distance in her eyes, until the mystery of their fathers was discovered, they couldn't go back to the way things had been. The sooner he proved it to her, the sooner he could kiss her.

Maeve didn't want her body to respond when Zeke placed his hands around her waist to lift her into the wagon. How could her body throb when he might be blood kin? It wasn't right. It made her feel filthy to even think about it.

Her mother had talked of families that went crazy from intermarriages. She wouldn't be the downfall of the strong Halsey family, even if she had any inclination to marry Zeke. Which she didn't. Not as long as he continued to mine for gold.

She bunched her skirt tight around her and tried not to touch him, but his broad shoulders rocked against her as they lumbered down the dirt road toward his family's mine. She hated mining. Hated even the thought of it. If her father hadn't been obsessed with finding gold and silver and becoming wealthy, she and her mother wouldn't have lived in squalor waiting for him to return and take them out of poverty. But when he did return, the money wouldn't last long, and he'd be gone again. Until the day he never returned.

"Nickel for your thoughts."

Maeve glanced at the man beside her. His intense gaze and sincere smile did little to help the thoughts banging around in her head.

"They aren't thoughts I'm ready to share." With you or anyone. He smiled, as if he'd expected that answer and clucked at the team of horses.

She'd never planned to think of a future with a man. Still had her doubts. No matter how hard she resisted Zeke, he came back, again, and again. In fact, he seemed to thrive on her rejection. It spurred him on to prove to her he cared. And she couldn't resist him.

Her gaze lingered on the mahogany hair curling up at the ends under his Stetson. His straight nose, coffee-colored eyes, and lips that perpetually tipped into a grin at the edges made her stomach flutter. At times his enthusiasm for life and good humor were infectious, but today—even his optimistic outlook couldn't shed hope on their predicament.

Maeve shook herself. Why did she even care if he was related? This was her excuse to keep him from courting her without hurting his male pride. She shook back her shoulders, sat straighter. What a profound opportunity this outcome provided. Yes. This was perfect. Zeke could remain in her life, but as a family member not an amorous suitor.

She glanced at him. He flashed a roguish smile, and a jolt of heat scorched her body. His dark eyes devoured her. How could she pretend she felt nothing for him when his gaze set her traitorous body on fire?

"You sure you don't want to talk about it. We've got plenty of time to discuss when you're going to come around and marry me."

"I don't think this trip will be quite that long."

He chuckled and she twisted away from him, staring at the pine-covered hills on either side of the valley they followed. The Halsey claim was northeast of Sumpter, a small community an hour's ride from McEwen. It would take the remainder of the day to travel to the mine, visit, and return her to the boarding house.

The higher elevation kept the air crisp most of the year. The early summer sun warmed her back and coaxed delicate, yellow buttercups to pop up among the tender spring grass.

Maeve breathed in the heavy pine scent. The tangy aroma brought back memories of a time when her father took her out far from town and taught her how to use a gun. That day was one of the few times she held dear to her. They shared a packed lunch, and he told her to never be afraid to use a gun. Some day it could be the difference between her walking this earth or leaving it.

Wiping at a tear, she stared at the trees as they

lumbered past. She never saw her father again after that day. *Why did you leave us, Daddy?*

"We're almost there." Zeke's strong hand rubbed her back. Maeve wiped at the tears and replaced the sadness with the anger she'd harbored the last ten years. Back in control, she placed her knees forward and watched the road they followed.

Only another mile or so and they'd be at the Halsey mine. Zeke had brought her here one time before. He constantly told her he wasn't a miner. That he only helped his brothers now and then. But it would take more than his words to make her believe he wasn't lured by the earth's treasures just like her no-good pa.

She'd spent a life time concealing the anger and pain that engulfed her on that cold winter morning when she and her mother had been evicted from their home. The only home she'd ever known. No one would know the agony she lived growing up believing her father never cared for her one minute and blaming herself for his disappearance the next.

"Hello!" A deep voice shouted.

She shook off the memory. Ethan, Zeke's oldest brother stood by a sluice box waving. A cabin nestled in pine trees a distance up the slope from the sluice box and clear stream. Farther upstream, a small shack sat beside two more sluice boxes. Mining paraphernalia leaned against the building. Between the two buildings sat a small barn.

Zeke tugged on the reins, stopping the matched horses pulling the wagon. He scrambled down from the wagon and around to her side before she had her skirt out of the way enough to step down on her own.

The dark, mischievous eyes smiling up at her broke Maeve's resolve to stay aloof. How was she to think of him as a cousin when he looked at her that way? Blast his hide. He grasped her around the waist, lifting her down like a child.

She swat at his hands when they remained at her waist. A deep chuckle rumbled in his throat as he faced Ethan.

"You got a minute to discuss something with Maeve and I?" he asked his brother, clasping her hand and leading her to the cabin.

"Yeah, Clay and Hank are off hunting." Ethan lifted his hat and wiped at the perspiration on his forehead.

She'd met all the brothers—even the married one, Gil, and his waif of a wife. All had the same chestnut hair, dark eyes, and strong stature. She found Ethan a rather intimidating figure. He was the oldest, the largest in height and breadth, and the one who could make them all take a step back when he roared an order. She'd also seen him nurse a young colt with the gentleness of a mother. He was a contradictory man, just like the one holding her hand.

They all entered the small cabin. A fireplace sat across from the door. A potbellied stove stood to the side of the cold hearth. Bunks lined the two sides of the building and a long, family-sized table filled the middle.

"Coffee?" Ethan plucked the pot from the potbelly stove.

"Not now," Zeke said, pulling out a chair for her.

"No, thank you." Maeve slid onto the chair and placed the tintype on the table.

Ethan sat down and picked up the replica of his parents. "How'd you get this?" he asked, raising his gaze from the tintype to her face.

"I took it to show Maeve what kind of people I came from." Zeke winked at her. "To help persuade her to think about marrying me."

Ethan exploded with laughter. "Brother, it would take more than a photo of our parents to make any woman want to be chained to you."

"Hey! I don't see women swarming around you!" Zeke grabbed the tintype and placed it on the table.

"Gentlemen," Maeve interrupted, "we came here for answers not a confrontation."

"What answers?" Ethan perched his elbows on the table and rested his chin on his clasped hands. His dark eyes searched her face. That was one of the reasons she refused Zeke's invites to the mine. His oldest brother seemed to see right inside a person. It unnerved her. The first time she visited he knew she didn't want anything to do with miners.

Clearing her throat, she proceeded. "I believe we are related."

Her proclamation wasn't laughed at. Ethan just continued to stare at her.

"How so?"

"She says her pa had this same tintype and that our pa was his brother." Zeke captured her hand on top of the table and squeezed. The gesture comforted and agitated her at the same time. She needed answers and support for which way her feelings should sway toward the man.

"So you think you're cousins?" Ethan looked directly at her. "That would be convenient."

Her heart jumped into her throat. How did he know her feelings? Did Zeke talk to him about her? Her face flushed with heat.

Zeke nodded his head. "Maeve thinks we're cousins and therefore shouldn't share the kind of feelings we do." He winked at her again and squeezed the hand he held. "But I say there has to be some kind of misunderstanding. Pa didn't have a brother, right?"

"As far as I know, Pa didn't have any brother that lived long enough to have a child." Ethan scratched his head. "But why would he say such a thing? Your father I mean."

"I wasn't hearing things. I remember thinking, how great it would be to meet family. When I asked if we would ever see them, he got a strange look on his face and said we couldn't." She glanced at the two men as resentment toward her father re-emerged. "Why do you think he would say a thing like that?"

"Because he didn't know who the people were in the tintype and made up a story. To have you meet them would prove him a liar." She heard derision in Zeke's voice.

Maeve didn't know why she cared, but he couldn't talk like that about her pa. She jerked her hand out from under his. "How do you know he lied? Maybe it was your pa who lied about having relatives." She may loathe her father but no one else could scorn him.

Zeke held up his hands. "I wasn't being disrespectful, just stating a thought."

"Zeke said your ma is still alive." Ethan pulled her glare from his brother.

"Yes. She lives in Baker City with her sister."

"Maybe you should take this tintype to her and see what she has to say." Ethan pushed the picture across the table.

"That's a great idea." Zeke stood. "Come on. I'll get you back to the boarding house. We'll head for Baker City first thing tomorrow morning."

"But I have school to teach." She stood, pocketing the tintype in her skirt.

"Can't you find someone to take over for the day or close the school?" Zeke couldn't help but smile when she gave him that schoolmarm look.

"No, I can't close the school because I want to take a trip to Baker City. What kind of an example would that make?" She scowled at him and turned on her heel.

He waggled his eyebrows at Ethan and followed her outside.

"Seems to me Mrs. White taught school before she married. Why don't you ask her to fill in for a couple days?" He caught up to Maeve before she climbed onto the wagon seat.

He grasped her waist to help her up.

"Let go of me," she said between clenched teeth.

"Why are you treating me like I've got a disease? Even if we find out we're cousins, I don't deserve to be cast aside like a two-legged pup." He dropped his hands and waited for her to slide over so he could climb up.

"Those our supplies?" Ethan asked, walking up to the wagon.

"Yeah. Hop in back. I'll drive down to the mine, and you can help unload it."

The wagon settled with Ethan's weight, and Zeke clucked to the horses. He'd felt Maeve stiffen when he said they were headed to the mine. Her feelings toward mines and miners didn't make any sense. One of these days he would sway her mind.

While they unloaded the supplies, she sat straight as an arrow on the seat. He knew she held little regard for her father who mined and left her and her mother destitute, but he wondered at her quick defense of the man. There was more to their history than she'd told him. He hoped her mother could shed more light on her father and the past Maeve used as a shield.

Chapter 2

Zeke tossed the reins of the horses around the hitching post in front of the boarding house. He still couldn't believe how hard it had been to convince Maeve to ask Mrs. White to fill in as teacher for a couple of days. They needed the one day to get to Baker City and one to travel back to McEwen. He hoped Maeve's aunt had room at her house to keep her niece overnight.

The sun barely peeked over the tree tops. Zeke looked up at the light shining in Maeve's room. She was awake and hopefully dressed. The sooner they headed out, the sooner they'd have some answers.

He climbed the three steps and raised his hand to knock. The door swung open. A beaming Mrs. White ushered him in.

"Maeve said you'd be here bright and early." The woman bustled around with extra energy. "I can't remember when I was so excited to greet a day!"

Zeke followed the woman down the hall to the

kitchen. The room smelled of bread, coffee, and bacon. The warmth was welcome after catching and saddling the horses in the predawn chill.

"Here you are." Mrs. White set a plate of food and coffee on the table. "Sit. Maeve already ate and will be down in just a minute."

"Thanks. I figured I wouldn't get anything in my belly until we stopped midday." He never turned down food. Something his brothers kidded him about all the time. He placed bacon between two pieces of bread and took a big bite, enjoying every chew.

The clomp of boots coming down the hall swung his attention from the food to the door. Maeve walked through, and he about choked on the bacon in his mouth.

She wore a calico blouse, dark split riding skirt, and a Stetson that hid half her face. Scuffed boots encased her feet. A single holster with a pearl-handled pistol hung against her left hip. She had the look of a woman who felt comfortable in the outfit.

"Why haven't I seen you wear this before?" He stood. The outlaw look appealed to him. He liked a woman with spit, hence the reason he'd been courting the feisty woman for a year.

"It isn't your normal school teacher attire." The grit in her voice made him wonder how often she dressed like this and why.

"Maybe not, but it looks good on you." He crossed the room. The desire to take her in his arms and show her his approval drove him forward, but she turned and headed down the hall.

"Ready?" she asked, pulling on gloves.

He stamped down his need and grinned. Waving to Mrs. White, he followed Maeve down the hall and out the door. Once they were outside, she didn't waste any time mounting a horse. She grabbed the horn, swinging up on its back as if she rode astride every day.

Why didn't I think of a trip like this sooner? Zeke mounted his horse and followed the feisty school teacher out of town. He would learn more about Maeve Loman from this two day trip to Baker City than he'd learned over the past year.

They trotted the horses out of town and into the valley they would follow all the way to Baker City. Zeke let her take the lead. He didn't mind riding behind, watching her stiffly held body sway with the horse. Maybe on this trip, he'd finally get a glimpse of the not-so-prim-and-proper school teacher she hid behind.

He kneed his horse up alongside her gelding. "Any chance you know how to use that pretty gun you have hanging from your hip?" He said it in jest, but realized his error when she turned a narrowed blue gaze on him.

"It just so happens, my father taught me one thing before he left us." She drew the pistol from her holster, leveled it, and cocked the hammer with her thumb. Glancing at him, a sly, crooked smile tipped her lips. She squeezed the trigger.

Peering past the spiral of smoke at the end of the pistol, he watched a pine cone topple off a limb.

She rode over to the pine cone, dismounted, and handed it to him.

He whistled and stared at the hole in the middle. "Not bad. You can watch my back any time."

Her dark eyebrows arched, and her mouth opened slightly.

Zeke wanted to lean down and kiss her.

When she found her voice, she asked, "You don't care I can outshoot most men?"

"As long as you don't use that gun on me, you can outshoot anyone you want." He couldn't keep from laughing. She expected him to be insulted because she was a better shot than him. She obviously hadn't been studying him like he studied her.

"I don't understand you. Most men would have a conniption if a woman shot better than them." She mounted her horse.

"Any man worth his salt knows his weaknesses and doesn't begrudge someone else who is better." He shook his head. "And sweetheart, you're better with a pistol than I am." He nudged his horse up alongside hers.

He caught her behind the neck with one hand and leaned in, capturing her lips before she could move away. Dang, she tasted good. When he felt the horses moving apart, he let her go. Her eyes remained closed, and she licked her lips. The quick rise and fall of her chest, made him grin. She could deny her feelings all she wanted, but he knew how he affected her, and he'd keep on plying her with kisses until she realized he wasn't going anywhere.

Zeke cleared his throat. "How come after all your talk about your pa being a no-good miner, you stuck up for him yesterday?" This was sure to change her disposition, but he'd been thinking on it all night and couldn't figure out her change of heart.

Her eyes snapped open. The glint in them told

him her mood had definitely changed.

"Why does it matter?" She started to jab her horse in the ribs. He caught the reins, holding her still. Her eyes flared with anger.

"Sweetheart, you have said nothin' good about your pa since I met you. Yet, when I called him a liar, you bristled up and defended him."

Maeve took a deep breath, letting the anger and air hiss out between her teeth. She should have known Zeke would call her on this. His quick mind had drawn her to him in the first place.

"I imagine there are times you say unflattering things about your brothers, yet if someone else were to say it, you'd jump all over them. It's the same for me." She twisted in the saddle, peering into his shaded face to see if he understood.

"So, even though you've called your pa every name a respectable school teacher would use, you don't want anyone else doing it. You are one contrary female."

She wanted to wipe that blasted grin off his too-handsome face. "I have pretty good reasons for calling him names, but that doesn't mean I don't have a few kind thoughts about him."

"Yeah, like what? All you've ever mentioned was how he left you and your ma to hunt for riches." His good humor turned to curiosity.

She turned her horse and started at a walk down the road to Baker City. "I remember when I was small, he took me fishing. We talked about how he planned to do more of that once we had a big house, and he didn't have to travel anymore."

"If you lived in this area, how come he traveled to find a gold mine?" There was that quick mind of his.

"We didn't live in this area. My mother and I moved here when I applied for the teaching job." She delved back through her memories. "I don't know where we lived when he took me fishing. I remember riding on a train at one point…" She hadn't really tried to remember the past. Most of it was too painful to keep in her memory.

"So when did you move out here? The train from the East didn't get to these parts until eighty-four." Zeke kept his horse even with hers. His frown and thoughtful expression meant he was calculating something.

"We lived in Oregon City until I started school." She would never miss all the rain. This area suited her.

"Were you born there?"

Maeve thought hard. "I don't know. I've never asked where I was born, never thought much about it."

"Well, it's something we need to ask your ma when we sit down and talk with her." He pulled his hat down over his eyes and set out at a trot.

She had a feeling he'd come up with more questions than her mother had answers.

Zeke glanced up at the sun. The yellow globe cast shadows directly under them. He'd stopped beside a lake to rest the horses and snack on the jerky and hardtack he'd packed.

He dismounted and waited for Maeve to do the same as he pulled a cloth-wrapped bundle out of his saddlebag. He handed the food to Maeve and led the two horses to the edge of the lake. Kneeling, he scooped water into his hands. His fingers numbed quickly from the first snow melt of the spring. He felt Maeve's presence before he heard her footsteps and breathing. She knelt beside him and scooped water.

Her shoulders shuddered before she raised the liquid to her lips. He watched her swallow and then wished he hadn't. Ever since setting eyes on the woman, he'd been as randy as a drunk cowhand. And ever since setting his sights on the lady, he'd stayed away from brothels.

If he could have dove into the lake without having to explain himself to the woman beside him, he would have jumped in fully clothed to relieve the ache in his loins.

He led the horses over to a patch of grass and tied the reins to a tree limb. The bundle of food sat on a large semi-flat boulder. He leaned against the rock and unfolded the cloth, pulling out a dried piece of meat. Chewing, he watched Maeve walk toward him.

She never gave any hint of her feelings for him. He'd kissed her enough to know, when she finally let him in, neither one would have regrets. He held out a piece of dried meat. She backed up to the rock and using her boot heels, shimmied up to sit on the boulder.

"Thank you." She accepted his offering and chewed on it, gazing out over the lake.

"You thought about what all you want to ask your ma?" Having grown up around his brothers he didn't like silence at a meal. Even a brief stop to eat.

"Some. I suppose once she answers, I'll have more come up." She glanced at him. "I suppose you want to be there when I talk to her?"

"I dang sure want to be there when you ask her about my pa." He touched her soft cheek with a finger. "I have answered all your questions about me truthfully. When are you going to let me learn about you?"

Her eyes softened for a moment before she turned away from his gaze and his touch. Why did she fight her feelings for him? She'd been running from her feelings since he met her.

"I-I, there are some things, I don't know the answer to. Like my father leaving us. I've thought about it so many times over the years. And—the only conclusion I can come up with is he didn't love us. And why what I felt for him wasn't a strong enough love to keep him."

Zeke moved around to look into her face. Tears shimmered in her eyes.

He gathered her into his arms. Before his eyes, she became the scared little girl whose father never returned. And now, he had a brief glimpse at why she fought his attention. She was afraid she couldn't love him enough.

He tipped her face. There was one way to show her how much he cared, that didn't need any words. He lowered his lips to hers. At first she held her mouth firm, denying him access. He slid his tongue across her lips, stroking, teasing. With a moan, her mouth opened, and she kissed him back with knee-buckling need.

His heart slammed into his ribs. This was the woman he knew she'd be when he started courting her. She tried too hard to be prim and proper. He knew a vixen hid under that prudish disguise.

Coming up for air, he noticed the stunned expression on her face. "That's what I've been waiting for."

She leaned away from him. "I'd rather you didn't kiss me until we figure out if our fathers were related." Her icy voice belied the blush on her cheeks.

"I'd do anything you ask, and you know it, but refraining from kissing your tempting lips—I'm afraid I'm not that strong." He flashed an apologetic smile and laughed when she slid off the boulder and marched to her horse. She swung up into the saddle and spurred the animal into a canter.

That was fine with him. He'd like to get to Baker City and get this cleared up. Maybe digging up her father's past would open her heart to him.

Chapter 3

Maeve let out a breath and raised her hand to knock on Aunt Geraldine's door. She held her hand in the air—inches from the wood. It bothered her Zeke had insisted on taking the horses to the livery while she announced their arrival. At the moment, she could use his self-assurance. In her rush to prove the Halsey brothers wrong, she neglected to tell Zeke she and her mother hadn't spoken since she took the teaching job in McEwen.

Gulping, trying to still her nervous belly, she rapped on the solid, wood door and dropped her hand to her side as if the door had been on fire. Maybe no one was home? Her spirits bolstered at the thought.

Light footsteps sounded on the other side. She wasn't ready to confront her mother.

Her feet slid back.

The door knob moved.

She couldn't catch her breath and took another step back.

The door began an inward swing—she spun on her heel and smacked into a hard chest.

"What—" Zeke's deep voice rumbled the chest under her hands and cheek. He grasped her upper arms and held her away. His calm gaze searched her face, lingering on her eyes.

She lowered her eyelashes, hiding the feelings she wasn't ready to share.

"Maeve? Is that you? And you've brought a beau!" Aunt Geraldine clapped her small hands before placing an arm around Maeve's waist and drawing her into the house.

Maeve threw a look over her shoulder and found Zeke smiling like he'd just found a gold mine. Blast! Now he'd play the part of her beau with zeal. She ground her teeth. He wouldn't be playing for long once Ma set him straight they were related.

"I can't believe you're here. And on a week day!" Aunt Geraldine drew her through the entry and into a parlor as inviting and homey as the petite woman drawing her deeper into the house. She stopped beside a small settee and looked up at Maeve with worried eyes. "You didn't lose your job did you?"

"No, Aunt Geraldine. I have something I need to ask Ma." Maeve glanced around the small, tidy parlor. It wasn't filled with opulent furnishings only the necessary items for a comfortable life. "Is she here?"

"Yes. Your mother is upstairs resting. I'll go get her." Aunt Geraldine stared at Zeke. A spark lit her faded blue eyes. She stuck out her hand. "I'm Maeve's Aunt Geraldine, and you are..."

Holding his Stetson in one hand, Zeke captured the woman's small hand in his empty one and bestowed his little old lady smile on the woman. She tittered and tipped her head sideways in a flirtatious manner. Now why couldn't Maeve have inherited some of her aunt's playful traits?

"I'm Zeke Halsey, Ma'am."

"I'm glad you brought my niece to see her mother. She has stayed away too long." With one last titter, the woman left the room.

Zeke took the spot on the settee next to Maeve. "What was that about on the porch?"

"I-I was having second thoughts." She pulled her hat off her head and smoothed the stray strands of hair back. Her hands shook.

"Why?" He stilled her hands and gazed into her eyes. Was that fear?

"Mother and I—we—"

"Argue about her father constantly." A small, frail-looking woman entered the parlor. Maeve must have took after her father. He'd never thought of her as anything other than strong.

He stood as the woman crossed the room.

She stopped in front of Maeve, placing a hand on the younger woman's shoulder. "I've missed you, Maeve."

The mother and daughter locked gazes, their eyes shimmered with unshed tears. He stood beside them, unseen, soaking in the resistance, sorrow, and acquiescence.

Mrs. Loman broke the spell. She wiped at a tear on her cheek and turned to him. "I'm Margaret Loman, Maeve's mother. And you are..."

"Zeke Halsey. A friend, and hopefully, some

day her husband."

The squeak and then exasperated sigh from Maeve made him smile. "She's fighting me on the last part."

Mrs. Loman glanced at her daughter. "I'd say he's a keeper if he can put up with your contrary moods."

The anger in Maeve's eyes brightened to the blue of a cloudless summer sky.

"Mother, we didn't come here for your con-gratulations on anything. We came to find out," she slipped the tintype out of a pocket in her riding skirt, "if this man was really a brother to father."

The older woman took a seat on the settee next to her daughter and held the tintype. "Where did you get this? Your father always carried it with him when he traveled."

"My sister-in-law found it in an outlaw's hide-out." Zeke watched the woman turn the object over and over in her hand before scrutinizing the front. She darted a look at him, then back at the image in her hand, and back at him.

"There's a strong resemblance here," she said, her gaze meeting his.

"Yes, Ma'am. Those two are my parents." He knelt next to Maeve. "Your daughter says your husband told her that was his brother. We need to know if that's the truth. Since as I stated before, I plan to make her my wife."

Maeve snorted. "That may be his plans, but I haven't decided if I want him in my life."

"Seems to me you don't have much choice. This man carries a pretty bright candle for you. I can see it in his eyes." Mrs. Loman patted her daughter's hand, then pointed to his father. "This man was not a blood relation."

Relief drained through him like water running through a sluice box.

Maeve straightened her back and grabbed the tintype. "Why did father talk of him like a brother and tell of jokes they played on people?"

"They worked together during the war."

He stared at the replica of his father. No one had ever said anything about Pa being gone. "My pa wasn't in the war. I know that for a fact."

"They weren't soldiers. At least not for either side." Mrs. Loman pulled a handkerchief out of her dress sleeve. She sniffed the dainty cloth and leaned back against the cushions.

"What do you mean?" Zeke sat on the arm of the settee next to Maeve. He'd been cleared of being a blood kin, but now his scalp tingled with uncertainty.

"Margaret, do you need to lie down?" Aunt Geraldine bustled across the hand-braided rug to her sister's side.

"What's wrong, Mother?" Maeve made the first attempt at contact with her mother since her arrival. The mother daughter relationship puzzled him. Having been left to fend for themselves, one would think they'd have a strong bond. The bond between his brothers strengthened after the deaths of their parents and younger brother. But he felt hostility oozing from the mother and daughter.

"I'm fine." Mrs. Loman brushed off her sister and daughter's hands and settled more comfortably on the settee. She looked at him. "What were you told of your father?"

"My brothers and I grew up in Sumpter. My father wasn't anywhere near the civil war when it happened. He was in Oregon country." The older woman's eyes opened in surprise, then narrowed. What did she know?

"You and your brothers may very well have grown up in Sumpter, but I can assure you this man," she tapped a finger over his father in the photo, "was part of the group my husband ran with during the war."

He scratched at the prickling hair on his scalp. There was no way his father could have been that far away during the war—Zeke was born during that time. And there was no denying he looked just like his brother's who all resembled their father.

"It can't be. There is no way my father could have been East during that time." He studied the woman. Dredging up the past wasn't helping her coloring any. Her already pale complexion was turning a pasty gray.

"Mother, how can you be so sure? Did you meet him? Or are you just going by what Father said. After all we know how reliable his word was." The contempt in Maeve's voice drew his attention. Her gaze rested on him. Was that concern he saw?

"I met the man one night. Your father thought I was sleeping, but it was close to your birth." Her eyes turned misty as she reminisced. "I didn't sleep well. I heard voices and went to the back porch. Your father and this man talked in hushed voices. I knew your father wasn't what he said he was, but he kept a roof over my head and made me feel special."

"What were they talking about?" Zeke cut into

her memories. It was rude, but he wanted answers just as desperately as Maeve.

"I didn't hear it all, but it had to do with an underground railroad. It wasn't until the war was over I put it all together. They were part of the group helping slaves out of the South."

Maeve sucked in her breath, and he shook his head in disbelief.

"I don't understand?" Maeve said, as he stared at the older woman. His father couldn't have been a part of something like that and not be missed. He knew his father was never gone more than a week at a time when he worked as a freighter to bring in more money.

"Not to be disrespectful, Ma'am, but there's no way my pa was there. He was never gone more'n a week at a time. That wasn't enough time to travel to the East and back let alone help some slaves get free."

Mrs. Loman looked him straight in the eyes. "That's what I know."

"When did we move here, Mother?" Maeve wrung her hands. He took one, hoping to give her support and muster up some for himself.

"A few years after the war, we moved to Philadelphia. Your father worked for a coal mine and was part of an organization. One day he came home, said we're going west. We were on the next train going as far west as it would take us and then by stage to Oregon City."

"That's where we were when he left us to go mining." Maeve clutched his hand as the bitter words tumbled from her pinched lips.

Mrs. Loman shot a sympathetic look at her

daughter and glanced at Zeke. "She's right. He left one day and never came back." The woman pulled a yellowed, sealed envelope from the folds of her dress. "I found this when I packed up my things to move in with Geraldine." She handed the envelope to her daughter.

Maeve felt the crispness of age as she took the paper. What could this be? She studied the handwriting on the outside.

If I should not return.

She stared at the slanted writing. Something told her it was from her father's hand. She glanced at her mother. The unshed tears in the older woman's eyes confirmed her thoughts.

"Why? Why didn't you show me this earlier?" Maeve slipped a trembling finger under the wax seal.

"You were so sure he left us for riches and greed. You wouldn't listen. Then when you stopped coming to see me altogether..." her words trailed off. Her mother dabbed at her eyes with the dainty handkerchief.

Maeve swallowed the lump in her throat. How was she to make up to her mother for all those years of not believing her? Yet, even as she had so vehemently told her mother they'd been abandoned, deep down she'd known her father wouldn't do that. Which only made it hurt all the more.

A wide, strong hand rubbed her back. Maeve glanced over her shoulder and into the sympathetic eyes of a man she'd become too dependent on.

Letting out a breath, she unfolded the letter and read:

Margaret, if you are reading this letter it means I have not returned. You have been a wonderful wife and mother. I could not have asked for anyone stronger or more faithful to be by my side through these years.

If you need anything, go see Barton at the High Stakes saloon in The Dalles. He'll help you. Tell Maeve, my treasure, I love her and to always cock the hammer with confidence.

Love, Brendan

Maeve wiped at the tears trickling down her cheeks. He hadn't abandoned them. Something happened. She handed the letter to her mother. How could she have so blindly assumed he left them? His love for them came through in the words of his note.

An arm encircled her shoulders, drawing her against Zeke's broad, hard chest. She didn't pull away. The anger and loathing she'd held onto released on a lengthy sigh. Tears slid down her cheeks. She felt weak and vulnerable and wanted his strong arms around her.

Letting years of pent up feelings escape, she burrowed deeper. Now, to hide the shame. Shame of having held those feelings for a man she remembered as loving. How could she have turned on him so drastically? And why?

She pulled out of Zeke's embrace, wiped her tears, and turned to her mother. The woman's tears ran silently down her pale cheeks.

"Why didn't you open that letter when you found it? Or at least contact me?" A warm hand rested on her shoulder. She shook it off. She remembered the reasons she'd thought the worst of her father. Little innuendos her mother had dropped along the years.

She narrowed her eyes, watching the woman. "You told me father left because he didn't want to see us anymore." Maeve pointed a shaking finger at her mother. "Why would you say something like that?"

The anger in her mother's eyes stunned Maeve. "Because you wouldn't stop chattering about your father. When he didn't return, you'd turn those big blue eyes on me and as much as accuse me of having chased him away. 'Daddy wouldn't leave me. Why didn't he come home?' Me. You knew he loved you more than me. When he was home for short periods of time, he'd spend every waking moment with you. I'd be left behind, washing his clothes, cooking his favorite meals, but you were the one he doted on. His little treasure."

Maeve leaned back against the solidness of Zeke. The hate and jealousy defiling her mother's face made her stomach churn. How could a parent hate their child so much? She wanted to turn and hide from the vileness.

"So you planted all those lies in Maeve's head," Zeke said. The vibration of his chest against her back comforted.

"I was sick of her mooning over a man who wasn't worth it."

"Why wasn't he worth it?" Maeve sat up straight. What would make her father not worth caring about?

"The rumors going around after he went missing." Her mother curled her lip in disgust. "I didn't want you to keep telling people your father was coming back, when they all watched us waiting for his return so they could put him in jail."

Maeve shook her head. "What do you mean jail?"

"Rumors spread he was part of a gang that held up a freight wagon loaded with gold headed to Canyon City." Her mother sat straight and glared. "I figured he was shot during the hold up and wandered off somewhere and died. Otherwise he would have come back for you."

"Why would you think your husband capable of being part of a gang?" Zeke asked. Maeve smiled at him, thankful he was there to help ask questions. Her mind reeled, and she didn't know what to ask next.

"He'd be gone for periods of time and return with enough money to keep us going until he'd head out again to make more." Her mother picked at the lace edge of the handkerchief.

"You never questioned him?"

"When I did, he said he had a gold mine, he and a partner were working." She glared at him. "But a gold mine doesn't bring in the same amount of money each time. I was bright enough to know that much."

Zeke's hand stretched out from behind Maeve. "I'd like to take a look at that letter, if you don't mind."

She took the letter from her mother and handed it to Zeke, watching him read it.

A smile lit his eyes, and he handed her the

letter. "Looks like you and me are headed to The Dalles."

Chapter 4

Maeve couldn't believe Zeke talked her into taking a sabbatical from teaching. And here they stood loading saddle bags with a change of clothes and food staples to get them to The Dalles. Knowing they weren't related, she wasn't sure why Zeke insisted on digging up information about her father.

"Sure you don't want one of us riding along?" Clay asked as Zeke tied a bedroll behind his saddle. She glanced at Zeke's brother. He was an older version of Zeke, by only a couple of years. Only his nose was a bit crooked. Zeke had yet to tell her how it happened.

"I don't think being on the trail with two Halseys will help my reputation. One's bad enough." She'd lied to Mrs. White when the woman asked about the sabbatical and stared straight at Zeke. Maeve told Mrs. White she was visiting relatives in Portland. Alone. How she would prefer to travel to The Dalles. She glanced at Zeke. The determined set to his jaw told her she wouldn't get very far without him. She didn't really want to travel alone on the trail, and if she had to have someone with her she couldn't think of anyone else she trusted.

"No, we don't need to pull any of you away from your duties. We can find The Dalles and talk to this man just fine." Zeke turned to Ethan, Clay, and Hank.

"What if you run into trouble?" Hank asked, handing him a canteen. The man didn't look so much worried as anxious to come along.

"I'll stand behind Maeve." He winked at her and her cheeks heated. "She's better with a gun than I am."

Ethan laughed and slapped him on the back.

"You sure you want to ride with such a coward?" Clay handed her a canteen.

"At least I know where he'll be ducking," she answered to his brothers' delight. They whooped it up, and she shook her head. What would it have been like to grow up in the cluster of so many siblings? And with parents who loved you equally? It still rattled her to learn of the jealousy her mother harbored and how it had kept them at odds all these years. A jealousy she hadn't even known existed. She'd just thought her mother irritable.

"Don't forget to flash that tintype around and see what you can find out about Pa." Ethan hadn't been as certain about their pa being in the Oregon territory all the time like Zeke.

"I still say it wasn't Pa working with Maeve's pa in the war." Zeke glared at his brother.

"We still have a few relatives back East. I'm sending them all a letter inquiring what they know about Pa and Ma. Might help us figure this out." Ethan put a hand on his brother's shoulder. "Too bad Pa isn't still alive to fill us in." All the brothers sobered. Ethan smiled. "If Pa was helping free the slaves, he was on the side of the right."

"I know, it just—it just doesn't seem like Pa to be sneaky with us. You'd have thought he'd have said something to at least you older boys." Zeke slapped Ethan on the back.

Maeve directed her attention to tightening the leather straps around her bedroll. After her pa left, she'd lost touch with sentimental feelings. Her mother ripped them out of her with lies and manipulation. And it took this last visit before she could look back on it all and see it for what it was.

Zeke stepped beside her, placing his hands on her waist. "Ready to go?" Peering into his eyes, she saw more questions than what he asked. They'd be on the trail at least four days by themselves to get to The Dalles. A shiver raced up her spine. It wasn't an omen, but rather, anticipation. Could she open her heart to this man, knowing what she now knew about the man she thought left her as a child? Or were her wounds too deep to heal?

"I can get on my own horse." She gently removed his hands from her waist and swung up into the saddle of the horse Hank loaned her for the trip. There were still lots of unanswered questions about her father and once they were out, Zeke could change his mind about how he felt about her. Best to keep their association uncluttered.

"Yes, Ma'am." Zeke winked at her and swung up onto his horse.

"Both of you be careful. You don't know what

you're getting into," Ethan said, placing a hand on Zeke's leg.

"We'll send a telegram when we have some answers." Zeke urged his horse forward and they were off. Maeve followed behind. There were so many questions that needed answered. The first one—was her father still alive or was he dead?

From the sound of his letter, he would have returned to them if he lived. Tears burned and she wiped a hand across her eyes. Of all the times for Zeke to glance over his shoulder. He stopped his horse, waiting for her to ride alongside.

"What's wrong?" He grasped the reins of her horse making it stop.

She sniffed and glared at him. How did she keep him at a distance when he seemed to sense all her moods?

"Listen, I'm in this with you. The more I know, the easier it will be to find answers." He placed a gloved hand under her chin, tilting it up, making her look into his eyes.

Blast! She preferred hiding from his gaze. He was the only person she'd ever let in. Only because she couldn't hide anything from him.

"Are you afraid we'll find out your pa didn't love you enough to come back or he's been dead all this time?"

She slapped at his arm, knocking away his touch.

A smile tipped the corners of his mouth. "That's my girl. I prefer you spitting to tearing up. We'll find the truth, and then we'll get married."

He said it with such conviction, she couldn't hold the guffaw.

"You're sure full of yourself. I don't plan on ever marrying." She nudged her horse forward. At this rate they'd never find any answers.

"We'll see." He fell in behind her, and she set her horse into a ground-covering, easy trot. They should make Canyon City after dark if they kept up this pace.

The streets of Canyon City were full of people even though the sun had settled nearly an hour earlier. Zeke shifted in his saddle, relieving his aching backside. It had been a while since he'd kept a horse at a good clip the whole day.

He stopped at the livery and eyed the people milling about.

"What's all the fuss," he asked when a boy came to claim their horses.

"Everyone's headin' to the Dance Hall." The boy smiled and scooted his feet in an awkward dance step.

"What's the occasion?" He untied his saddle bags and saw Maeve already had hers over her shoulder.

"Jensen and Miss Holly finally got hitched." The boy smiled. "They been shinin' one another for years."

Zeke laughed. He hoped it didn't take years to win over the woman standing beside him frowning.

"What's the best hotel in town?" He handed the boy a silver dollar for the care of the horses.

"Try the Golden Eagle. It's down that way about three blocks. Can't miss it."

He nodded and settled Maeve's elbow in the palm of his hand.

"I thought we wouldn't need a room until The Dalles," she said, only loud enough for him to hear.

"I'll pay for a room for you. No sense sleeping on the ground until we have to." The way he felt about the woman, it was better to have a wall between them than nothing but air.

She stopped and faced him. "I'll not be a kept woman."

He couldn't keep the corners of his mouth from tipping into a smile. Dang, but he loved it when she was all fired up.

"You aren't a kept woman. The only way you'd be a kept woman was if I snuck into your room during the night."

The half moon shone bright enough he watched the color on her face deepened. "This isn't the place to discuss my yearnings." He clamped onto her elbow and continued down the street. The boy was right. The doors of the Golden Eagle stood wide open with brightly lit lanterns illuminating the interior.

The building was of average size. A small entry opened to the counter on one side and the stairs to the rooms on the other. Zeke stepped aside, gesturing Maeve to enter. He followed and crossed to the counter where a dapper-dressed man stood.

"We'd like two rooms for the night," Zeke said as the clerk slid his gaze from the top of Maeve, lingering at the blouse stretched taut across her breasts, and down to her dusty boots.

Zeke slapped the counter, jolting both the clerk and Maeve. Jealousy wasn't something he

was in the habit of feeling. But the man's eyes rak-
ing over his woman sparked the anger he'd held off
since learning of Maeve's painful childhood.

"And I want the rooms adjoining." He didn't
even bother to keep the steel out of his voice. He
wanted the man and anyone else within earshot to
know the woman was off limits.

Maeve clutched his arm, stood on her toes, and
whispered, "What's wrong?"

In the same loud, steel voice he said, "Just
making it clear you're to be left alone."

He felt her drop back to the flat of her feet.
When the clerk spun the register, he signed his
name and handed the quill to Maeve to sign. That
brief instant of giving her control rewarded him
with an innocent smile. She'd smiled at him before,
but always with reservations. As though afraid to
enjoy his company or let him know she enjoyed
something he did for her.

The clerk slid the keys across the counter. He
grabbed both of them.

Hearing Maeve's stomach growl, he asked,
"How much longer will the restaurant be open?"

"You have half an hour," the clerk retorted, not
allowing his gaze to stray.

"Let's dump this stuff in the rooms and come
back down." He once again captured her elbow,
escorting her up the stairs. Their footsteps echoed
down the uncarpeted hall as he found the door to
her room. He handed her the key, waited for her to
enter, and moved to the next door.

He walked into the room and found her standing in the open door joining the two rooms.

"What was that all about with the clerk?" she

asked, not taking a step into the room. "And why the joining rooms?"

"I didn't like the way he looked at you, and I wanted to make it clear no one was to touch you." He dropped his saddlebag over the straight back chair and approached her.

"H-how was he looking at me?"

"You didn't notice his eyes—lingering." He'd made it a rule to not look at her attributes when she looked at him.

"No." She scowled. "Where were they lingering?"

He moved his hand back and forth in front of her breasts, but kept his eyes locked on her face. "Here."

Her face flushed a deep red. "Why?"

"Men tend to be interested in," he cleared his throat, "that part of a woman."

He knew she hadn't been sparked by anyone other than him, but he didn't realize she hadn't noticed the way men looked at her.

"Do you," she waved her hands in front of her, "look here?"

He tried to appear apologetic, but he wanted to pull her into his arms and taste her. "There have been a few occasions, I've looked."

She ducked her head.

"Oh, don't do that. There's nothing to be ashamed about. You can't help you have the body a man drools over."

Her head snapped up. The innocence and questioning in her gaze snapped his resolve. He pulled her against him, tipped her head back, and captured her soft lips under his. She didn't struggle. When he tilted his head and ran his tongue along the seam of her lips, she sighed. Her hands slid up his chest and gripped the back of his neck.

Maeve had never listened to the other girls talk about boys and as they grew older—men. She'd always stayed to herself. She knew how cutting women could be to one another, well at least her mother to her. When Zeke said he looked at her, heat radiated to her toes. She fought the desire to touch him. Only he took the matter into his own hands, and she could acquiesce without him knowing she had wanted it before he embraced her.

She opened her mouth, allowing him entry. Shivers of delight danced through her. Pressing her body against his, she felt his solidness and warmth.

When he tipped his head back, she ran her hands down his shoulders, squeezing the hard muscles in his arm. He had the strength of two men. She'd witnessed it watching him build the Gantry house.

She loved that he was strong. Yet, she knew he would never use his strength to make her do anything she didn't want to. And he would answer her questions.

She pulled out of the kiss. "Why don't you want anyone else touching me?" She peered up into his face.

"I thought you'd figured that out by now." His dark eyes glimmered with heat as his mouth descended on hers again. He straightened, clasping her to him and dangling her feet off the floor. If he hadn't embraced her, she would have melted to a puddle on the floor. His kiss boiled her insides and set off yearnings she couldn't explain.

Her stomach rumbled.

He dipped his tongue through her lips and pulled back, sliding her down his long, hard body. She wobbled a little. He clutched her against him. Her face flattened against a dusty, flannel-clad chest.

"You need food. And I need space." He kissed the top of her head and stepped back.

She leaned against the door jamb. She'd just sent him a message, she'd been avoiding. Blast! But it was so good. Nothing had ever set her on fire or made her feel safe as being in Zeke's arms.

"I'll go order. You can freshen up and join me." He smiled nonchalantly, but his gaze roamed over her face like he'd never seen her before.

"I'll come with you." She took a step away from the wall.

"Umm...you might want to tidy up your hair a bit." His grin and the gleam in his eyes made her hand fly up to feel her hair.

She'd braided her long stringy locks that morning, but she could feel the loose strands hanging around her face. She ducked back into her room and pulled a hairbrush and small mirror out of her saddlebag.

Her face was flushed, her lips wet and swollen, and her hair—had been through a wind storm. She pulled the ribbon from the end of her braid and ran the brush through it. With shaking fingers, she pulled it up on the sides, using a pair of combs she'd tossed in on a whim.

Once the task was done, she pressed a hand to her trembling stomach. She and Zeke had kissed before. A chaste kiss on the cheek or a quick peck on the lips. However, what had just transpired... Oh, my! No one had ever told her kissing could be so wonderful. Her breath came in little spurts as she recalled the time she spent in Zeke's arms and the taste and feel of his lips.

Her stomach rumbled again. She better hurry or he'd come back up looking for her. Glancing at the door between their rooms, she crossed the room and locked the door. One moment of rapture in Zeke's arms was all she could take in one day.

Zeke sat in the restaurant watching the food he ordered get cold. The table was the right size for an intimate dinner and set back in the corner. He scanned the other customers. By their dress and boisterous talk, he pegged them for traveling salesmen. There was only one other couple in the small dining room. The elderly couple had smiled at him when food for two was delivered.

What was taking Maeve so long? Just as he started to go look for her, she stepped hesitantly into the restaurant.

The few occupants lingering over their meals in the small dining room looked her way. He saw the accessing glances and smiled smugly when her gaze found him. She favored him with a shy, but beguiling smile.

Standing, he held out a chair for her. She was still dressed in her dusty riding skirt and blouse, but she'd done something with her hair. The dark, straight strands fell midway down her back. She'd pulled the sides up, holding them with some feminine looking doodads.

"Now, I know what took you so long," he whispered, pushing her chair in and leaning close.

"Was it that long?" She peered at him from under half-mast eyelashes. He didn't think she knew how to flirt or be shy. From the first moment he met the woman, she'd proved her independence and starch.

"Yes, your food is getting cold." He picked up a fork and started eating. Glancing at the woman beside him, he smiled as she took a bite of potatoes and grimaced. "Told you it was cold."

"I'm not complaining. The jerky we had at mid-day didn't last." She scooped another bite and continued cleaning her plate.

After a slice of apple pie, she leaned back in her seat, a satisfied lift to her lips. He watched her unabashedly.

Her eyelids started to droop. "Come on, you need sleep." He took her hand, helping her to her feet. "We won't have this nice of accommodations the next couple of nights."

Once she stood, he felt her pull away. She was the most contrary woman he'd ever come up against. Earlier she kissed him, making him weak-kneed, and now she pulled away like he had the fever. He wasn't going to make a scene, here, in the restaurant. They could talk this out upstairs in their joining rooms. His heart thumped faster. Maybe even share some more kisses.

At her door, he started to follow Maeve into the room.

"Excuse me. Your room is next door," she said, putting a hand on his chest, holding him out.

"I wanted to talk to you for a bit. And I can

just scoot on through the joining door when we're done." He smiled and tipped his head in an attempt to capture her lips.

The quick little devil turned her head and gave him a shove. In his distracted state, he found himself standing in the hall. He smiled. So we're back to the chase once again. He hurried to his room and grasped the knob on the joining door.

Chapter 5

The knob didn't turn, and the door didn't budge.

"Maeve, let me in. We need to discuss things." He knocked on the door gently. Nothing. He placed an ear against the wood and heard the soft rustle of clothing. He hardened imagining Maeve shedding her clothes. Thump, thump. That would be her boots landing on the floor.

He knocked again and listened. The slap of bare feet on wood drew near the other side of the door. He leaned back, ready for the door to open.

"Whatever we need to talk about can be discussed on our long ride tomorrow." Her whisper sent a coil of heat straight to his loins and aching body part.

"But-"

"Good night, Zeke." The finality and softness in her voice deflated his ego, yet didn't squelch his desire.

"I don't want to wait until tomorrow," he

growled.

"I'm not opening the door. Unless you plan to yell and let the whole place hear what you have to say, you can wait." The sound of her bare feet retreating across the floor and the creak of the bed as she climbed on told him the conversation had ended.

The dang woman kissed him like a wanton woman earlier and now was being as prudish as a preacher's daughter. He undressed and climbed into bed. One thing was for sure, he wasn't going to forget the way she kissed him. In fact, he looked forward to more occasions to hold and kiss Miss Loman.

"What if this Barton fellow isn't even at the saloon?" Maeve couldn't shake the feeling they were wasting time. Her father had disappeared over ten years ago. They may never run into any-one who even knew him.

"We'll keep asking around until we find him." Zeke had dropped back to ride alongside her when they slowed the horses to a walk.

"This could be a useless trip. I really shouldn't have let you convince me to take a sabbatical. I need the money I get from teaching." The blinding evening sun finally ducked behind the mountain in the distance.

"I understand your need for independence and teaching gives you that. But one of these days, someone," he waggled his eyebrows, "like me, would be happy to make you his wife and you won't have to teach."

"What if I wanted to continue teaching?" She wasn't giving in to his insistence they get married, but it was a tempting thought, one that kept her awake last night reliving his kisses.

"Then you can keep teaching." He reached over, cupping her chin. "I want you to be happy. That's all."

The sincerity in his eyes brought a lump to her throat. She swallowed and asked, "How do you know I'm not happy the way things are?"

"We'll stop here for the night." He walked his horse off the freight road and over to a tall, leafy stand of cottonwood and clumps of dogwood beside a stream.

Maeve dismounted. She scanned the area. They were far enough from the road no one would know they were camped if they doused the fire before they went to sleep. She'd heard of gangs robbing the freight wagons. Would they also rob two people who had nothing of worth? She shuddered. This would be her first night of ever sleeping without a roof.

A hand rested on her shoulder and she jumped. His deep chuckle lit her fuse.

"That isn't funny! I don't appreciate you sneaking up on me."

"I wasn't sneaking. Anyone could have heard me walk up, I wasn't pussyfootin'." Zeke slid his hand down her arm and back up. His strength ebbed into her. They were safe here. He wouldn't let anything happen to her.

"I have a confession." She bit her bottom lip, wondering if it was a good idea to let him know she was scared. If jumping when he put a hand on her didn't already give him the idea, he was denser than she thought.

"You've only been stringing me along because it was so much fun?" He pulled her around to face him. The wiggling eyebrow and crooked grin revealed he was fooling with her.

"No, I string you along because you're a contrary man. My confession is—I've never slept outside."

He scanned her attire. "I was sure with as worn as those clothes look, you'd took to the trail more than once."

"Well, I have traveled, but I always stayed in a stage stop or building of some sort."

He grinned and his eyes danced with merriment. "I'm traveling with a greenhorn."

"Hey, watch who you call names!"

"Stake out your horse, and I'll show you how to build a fire." He led his horse to the water.

She did the same, allowing the mare to drink her fill. When the horse raised its head and turned from the stream, she loosened the cinch and placed the saddle, saddlebag, and blanket on the ground. She took the bridle off and tied the horse to a tree where a patch of grass was within easy reach.

Watching Zeke, she set her saddle like he did and propped her saddle bag up against it, draping the whole thing with the blanket.

"Round up some dry sticks," he said, placing rocks the size of a head in a circle.

She scurried about under the trees picking up the fallen branches. Her arms were loaded when she returned to the fire pit. Zeke broke the sticks and stacked them, stuffing dried grass and a small slip of paper in the middle. He took a small, tin match safe out of his pocket and lit the grass.

A wispy tendril of smoke undulated toward the darkening sky. The flames grew, licking and snapping. He pulled a coffee pot from his saddlebag and filled it with water.

"What can I do?" Maeve asked feeling awkward. She was acceptable in the kitchen, but nothing like Mrs. White or Aunt Geraldine. She'd never done more than heat up water for coffee while out on a ride. Why did riding around alone during the light of day not bother her, but being with Zeke in the dark scared the wits out of her? Not that he would hurt her or let anyone else harm her, but she wasn't prepared for the attraction that seemed to grow with each hour they spent together.

"You could pull a loaf of bread out of my saddle bag." He handed her a long, double-sided, sharp knife that appeared out of nowhere. She grasped the worn antler handle. The weight of the knife pulled her hand into her lap.

"This weighs as much as my gun," she commented, rummaging around in the saddlebag he'd indicated.

"It's a precision weapon, just like your gun only quieter and unobtrusive." The hardness in Zeke's eyes divulged he'd used it on more than one occasion to either kill or keep from being killed. Shivers riffled down her spine. When he'd made fun of her being a better shot, she never gave a thought to him having a weapon. She'd never witnessed him pushed to draw this knife. She was sure it never left his person just as her gun was always within arm's reach, even at school. Some of the parents would have a conniption knowing the school teacher carried her gun to school with her every day in her lesson bag.

She didn't know why she felt the need to always have it handy. Other than her father's warning to always keep it close. He taught her how to handle a gun and insisted she never forget how to shoot. That was why she made a point to ride out every Sunday after church and practice. Did he know trouble was coming? And did she practice because it was a warm memory and connection to him?

"You going to cut me a slice of that bread or stare at it all night?" The humor in Zeke's voice brought her back from her melancholy thoughts.

"I figure you can wait a minute or two. You aren't going to waste away to nothing." The knife slipped through the crust like it was warm butter rather than a solid substance.

"It's not that I'm starving, I'd like to open this can of beans."

She cut several slices and handed the knife back to Zeke handle first, being careful not to touch either side of the shiny blade.

Fascinated, she watched him place the curved tip of the knife at the edge of the top of the can. He hit the end of the handle with his palm, tapping the point through the metal like a needle sliding through fabric. With precision and little effort he cut around the top of a can and removed it. She never wanted to be on the pointed end of that knife.

Zeke placed the can of beans next to the fire. "It shouldn't take long for the beans to heat up. Be a minute before the coffee's ready, too." He sat on his backside and leaned against his saddle which sat conveniently nearby. His long legs, crossed at the ankles, stretched out beside the fire.

He looked at home and peaceful.

She picked her saddle up, placed it by the fire like his, and sat, leaning against the contraption like he did. It wasn't bad. Not like sitting on a settee, but it propped her back. She placed her hands behind her head and leaned back. This she could get used to. No papers to correct, no assignments to get ready for the next day. Just her, the stars…

"Hey, don't go to sleep, you have dinner to eat and questions to answer." Zeke pulled the can out of the fire and divided the beans alongside the slices of bread on two tin plates.

He handed her a plate, fork, and cup of coffee as she watched his chiseled face the best she could in the growing darkness and flicker of the fire.

The beans were hot. She blew on them, keeping her head downcast, hiding from his probing eyes. What could he possibly have left to question her about?

When he bent to the task of eating, so did she. Nothing ever got settled on an empty stomach. She ate slowly, sopping up the juices with the bread to make the meal last longer.

A contented sigh drew her gaze from her plate to the man lounging against his saddle. His raised arms pillowed his head. His hat tipped forward hiding his eyes and revealing a satisfied smile curving the corners of his full bottom lip.

She stood and moved around the fire to pick up his plate. He caught her wrist so fast, she yelped. With a swift move, she landed on Zeke's lap holding a plate and fork in each hand.

"Just the way I like it," he said, capturing her head in between his hands and drawing her toward him.

She started to sputter about propriety when his lips descended on hers—hot, soft, and gentle—all thoughts fled. His hands slid up into her hair, knocking her hat behind her. He cradled her head like a cherished object. The kiss deepened, her heart thrummed, and her hands relaxed. The dishes dropped to the ground before she wound her arms around his neck, pressing her body against his.

Energy warmed her in places she'd never experienced before. The pressure of his hard chest against her breasts made them ache. She pulled back and shook her head. What was happening?

His lips sought hers, but she pulled back again. She was alone in the middle of nowhere with a man who made her do things she wouldn't normally do. This had to stop.

She pushed against his chest with her hands, making space between their heated bodies. "No. Please, stop."

Zeke allowed her to pull away. He'd never do anything to make her feel pressured. When she'd reached down to pick up his plate, he couldn't help himself. He'd been taunted by her lips all day.

He raised his hands in surrender and let her scramble off his lap. Every time he kissed her, she tasted better. And stayed in his arms longer. He smiled. With time, she'd never leave his arms. Not if he hadanything to say about it.

She huffed to the edge of the stream and

washed the plates with handfuls of sand. He liked how the riding skirt pulled taut across her backside. If she knew the view she gave squatting by the stream, he'd bet she wouldn't be doing it. He chuckled and pulled his hat down over his eyes. If she caught him gawking at her, she'd give him a tongue lashing. He didn't want her riled up just yet. He had some questions to ask. If she didn't spit out some answers tonight, she better by tomorrow night cuz the following day, they'd be in The Dalles and looking up this fella Barton.

Maeve placed the dishes on her saddlebags and unfurled her bedroll. He chuckled when she placed it a ways away on the opposite side of the fire.

"You're gonna get cold way over there by yourself," he offered, tossing the remains of his coffee out into the darkness surrounding them.

"I'll be fine." She sat on one blanket and pulled the other over her as she lay down, pulling her felt hat down over her face.

Zeke tossed another stick on the fire and stood. He stretched before heading into the trees to relieve himself. About the time he was thinking of a way to put his bedroll beside hers a coyote let loose a string of yips. Another joined and pretty soon it sounded like about a dozen cavorted around chasing something.

When he got back to camp, Maeve stood, wadding her blankets in her arms.

"Shouldn't we climb a tree or something?" she asked, scanning the grove of trees they'd camped under.

"Why would you want to do that?" He tried hard to keep the laughter out of his voice. For putting on a tough front, she sure scared easily.

"So the coyotes don't attack us during the night."

"I've never slept in a tree, and I've never been attacked by a coyote. They're after their dinner."

"Yeah, us."

That did it, he couldn't hold it in. He burst out laughing and it garnered him a scowl.

"This isn't funny!"

"I can't," he sucked in air, "I can't believe you're afraid of coyotes. I've seen you stare down men who are more frightening than a pack of mongrels."

She stood, clutching her blankets and peering into the darkness.

"Come here," he motioned her toward him.

Her eyes narrowed, and she shook her head.

"I promise not to touch you. If it makes you feel better you can sleep between the fire and me. No coyote will try to get you then." He couldn't suppress the snicker.

She stomped over to him, smacked him in the shoulder, and spread her blanket on the ground where he indicated. "You have to stay this far away." She walked past him and drew a line in the dirt with the heel of her boot.

Zeke looked at it and shook his head. "That's a long way from the warmth of the fire." He walked behind the line. "And it leaves a good space for a coyote to sneak in between us."

A chorus of yips couldn't have come at a better time. Her head just about spun off her shoulders as she peered into the trees and shadows beyond the fire's glow.

"You can sleep just this side of the line." Maeve plopped down on the blanket and turned her back to him.

He grinned and unrolled his blankets half way between the line and the curled up woman. She might want him to keep his distance, but the fire was on the other side of her, and he wasn't going to lose sleep because he was cold.

<h1 style="text-align:center">Chapter 6</h1>

Faint light filtered through the leaves over-head. Maeve ducked her cold nose under the blanket and snuggled deeper into the warmth sheltering her body.

She was outside, under trees. Her mind snapped awake. A large, male arm wrapped around her middle, snuggling her tighter against her warm cocoon.

She knew who the arm belonged to. A man who made her forget proprieties. She grasped the flannel-clad restraint, prying it from her person. When she started to roll out from under, another arm snaked under her, drawing her back against his hard body.

"I'm not ready to get up." Zeke's deep voice rumbled against her back.

"I am," she said, working to get loose from both arms encircling her. The cotton blouse she wore rubbed her breasts as his flannel clad arm held her hostage. Every inch of her body tingled.

"Hold still. You'll make me have to lay here longer." The undercurrent in his words caused her to stop. What did he mean?

"Just let me up, and you can lay there as long as you want." She tried prying his arms loose again. This time they granted her freedom.

She grabbed her blankets and rose. Maeve didn't dare look down. Her heart pounded so strong it drummed in her ears. How long had she slept cradled against his body? She shivered. His warmth had enveloped her, not only giving her heat but safety.

Rolling the blankets, she walked to her saddle. She tied the bedroll to the back of the saddle and snagged the coffee pot sitting next to the dead fire. "Get the fire going, and I'll bring some water up for coffee."

When he didn't respond she looked his way. Was that pain on his face as he started to rise? Did he have an affliction she wasn't aware of?

"Did you sleep on a rock during the night?" she asked, bending to give assistance.

Zeke swiped at her. "Go away. You're the cause of my stiffness this morning."

She straightened and stared at him. How could she cause him stiffness? He slept on the hard ground and that wasn't her fault. Well, in a way it was. He traveled with her to find answers to her father's past.

He rolled away from her and stood. Once on his feet, he grabbed the coffee pot out of her hand. "You gather more sticks for the fire. I'll get the water."

She watched him stiffly walk toward the

stream. A man of his age and lifestyle should be used to sleeping on the ground.

Zeke returned to the camp with a filled coffee pot. In the distance, he spotted Maeve bending, retrieving dried sticks. He turned from the sight. He'd splashed cold, stream water on his face and back of his neck to relieve his stiff cock. Then the sight of her bending over—he moaned and turned to his saddlebag to pull out the pouch of coffee grounds.

He stirred the coals in the fire pit. Some charcoal glowed when air reached it. He placed a handful of dried grass on the glowing orange remnants and blew, making a small flame.

Sticks tumbled to the ground beside him, and Maeve walked away. He grabbed several and continued feeding the flame until a hot fire singed his cheeks.

He looked around. Maeve had the horses down by the stream. When she brought them back to the camp, the coffee had boiled. He dumped a cup of cold water into the pot and poured two cups.

"What are we eating this morning?" she asked, sitting on the ground across from him.

"That bread from last night." He reached down to his boot and pulled out his knife as she turned to the saddlebag. When she held the bread, he handed her the knife, hilt first.

"Have you ever killed anyone with this?" She slipped the blade into the bread, carving even slices. He watched her use the knife with respect. She put two slices together and handed them to him.

"Why do you want to know?" He took the offering and continued to study her.

"You're avoiding answering me, so I take that as a yes." She examined the knife. "Why do you keep it in a boot sheath rather than on your belt?"

"Because honest men don't use weapons for defense and dishonest men deserve to be surprised."

She didn't even flinch at his answer, only nodded her head and chewed on the bread. "Makes sense."

"Why do you wear your gun everywhere? Even to bed?" He'd wondered if she'd take the holster off when she went to sleep last night. She hadn't and slept as though she'd done it before.

"Out here you never know who might try to take advantage of a woman." She narrowed her eyes and he laughed.

"I wasn't taking advantage of you. I was taking advantage of your heat. You blocked the fire." And he couldn't resist the way her body curled so perfectly against his. He blew out air and pried his thoughts away from the way she felt or he'd be stiff again. He could tell from her insinuations earlier, she didn't have a clue about men and their needs. Her mother had done a real poor job of bringing her daughter up in the world. He wasn't sure the best way to teach her. Explain or show. Damn. There he went again. Thinking things he shouldn't.

"And I wasn't the one who was scared of the coyotes." He grinned when she glared at him.

"I won't be tonight, I can assure you." She stuffed the last of the bread in her mouth and stood. Bending, she picked up her saddle and hauled it over to her mare.

He jumped to his feet and helped her place the saddle on the horse's back. Their hands touched, and they both stopped. He stared into her eyes. He'd never been one to let a chance go by. Leaning in, he brushed his lips against her soft mouth.

She started to pull back. He placed a hand behind her head, to keep her sweet lips under his. After holding her during the night and keeping his body restrained, he had to at least experience the taste one more time.

A sigh escaped her parted lips, and he hesitantly deepened the kiss.

Maeve leaned against him. The sensations of his mouth on hers, his hand cradling her head, and his body against hers made her feel alive and cherished. No one had ever wanted her. Not her mother. Maybe her father. But why had he left if he did? This man, kissing her and making her knees weak, had left a job to help her discover her father's past.

And he wanted her. He groaned and pulled her firmly against him, his hands roaming up and down her back, forming her to him. The heat of his hands and the firmness of his body against hers made the juncture of her legs throb. It was a sensation unlike anything she'd encountered.

Her hands, drifted up his chest. The fuzzy flannel beneath her palms contrasted with the solid muscle underneath. Her hands tingled. What would they do if she touched his skin?

He shifted and something hard rubbed between his lower region and her lower body. She slid a hand down to see what it could be. He had a stick in his pants! She jumped back and he groaned.

"W-why do you have a stick—in-in-" she couldn't finish, just pointed to his crotch.

His smile was tight, and he winced as he walked away from her horse. "Tighten the cinch. We'll discuss it as we ride." His arthritic gait resembled earlier when he'd risen from the ground.

Zeke looked over at Maeve. They'd traveled in silence most of the morning. He'd explained the feelings a man gets and what happens to a certain appendage. She'd asked a few questions, but spent most of the time just staring ahead as they trotted at a steady pace toward The Dalles.

He stopped his horse under a large cottonwood by a stream. "Let's give the horses a drink and a rest," he said, dismounting and leading his horse to the water.

She dismounted and stretched. This had to be taking a toll on her backside and thighs. He was pretty sure as a teacher she didn't get a chance to do this much riding.

He loosened the cinch and let the horse graze. Scanning the area, he took a seat on the ground. Maeve stood a short distance away, looking perplexed.

"What're you thinking about?" he asked, motioning for her to take a seat next to him.

She glanced at the spot, then at his face. "I don't want to cause you any, you know, problems."

He laughed. "You can sit next to me. I'm not going to explode."

Cautiously, she lowered to sit about two feet from him.

"You don't have to act any different around me. Just know that there will be times, like this morning when I can't control the urges I have for you." He pulled off his gloves and cupped her chin in the palm of his hand. "I only have these urges because I care for you."

Her eyes glistened. The uncertainty he saw in their depths, squeezed his chest.

"I will never touch you intimately unless you want it. As much as it will hurt, and I don't mean just physically, I will never touch you other than kissing and hugging unless you ask."

Maeve peered into his dark brown eyes. She was still trying to make sense of the information he'd told her. How had she become twenty-two and not known about a man and a woman—the intimacies? How could her mother have let her grow up being so naïve? What if she had run into a man who didn't have Zeke's good qualities?

She gasped thinking what could have happened to her, not knowing this information.

"What's wrong? Do you hurt somewhere?" He waggled his eyebrows. "I could rub it for you."

She shook her head. "I just thought...what if I ran into a man who, unlike you, didn't care about my feelings. I could have been," she gulped, "compromised." She studied his face. Anger flashed in his eyes then disappeared.

"I'll never let anyone touch you."

"But you aren't always around." She reached out to him. "I do enjoy your company, but Zeke, you can't always be here protecting me."

"If some man tries to touch you, shoot him." The coldness of his words made her shiver.

"I-I can't shoot every man who touches me. I'd be in jail."

"I don't mean literally. I mean, if it doesn't feel right." He put a hand on her shoulder and slid it down her arm. "Does that bother you?" he asked.

Warmth rolled down her arm in the wake of his hand. "No. It-it makes me feel safe."

He scrunched his brow. "What about Albert Simmons? Has he ever touched you?"

What did the nasty old man who was always begging food and money have to do with this conversation? "No, I don't believe he's touched me."

"But what kind of feelings do you get when you see him?"

"The hair on my arms tingle, and my lip curls."

"That's what I'm talking about. If a man touches you and you have that kind of feeling—don't let them get any closer. And if they do,do what you have to." Again, that cold disregard for life. Why had she not seen this side of him before?

"Come on, I want to make good time today, so we get into The Dalles before dark tomorrow." Zeke held out his hand to help her up.

She accepted the offer and stood. He stood so close, her breasts brushed against his chest. His head dipped, and his lips descended.

The heat of his kiss scorched through her body. If she continued to allow him kisses and his hands to roam over her body, as they were now, would they end up having the intimacy he spoke about earlier? For some reason, the thought didn't scare her, but rather elicited excitement.

A horse nickered, and he pulled away. Maeve wobbled a bit, then snapped straight at the sound of hooves and wheels.

Zeke collected the horses and handed the reins of her horse to her as a freight wagon plodded along the road a short distance from their resting spot.

When they were both mounted, he leaned toward her. "Just so you know. I would never compromise you."

"I know." She flashed him a smile. "And I'd never compromise you." She kicked her horse into a trot and laughed as she sped down the road catching and passing the freight wagon. Waving at the driver, she felt a light-heartedness she didn't remember ever feeling. Surely, she did when she was younger, before her father's disappearance.

The sound of an approaching horse reminded her of the importance of this trip: to discover the pasts of her father and Zeke's, and to learn if there was a future for herself and the man riding up behind her.

Chapter 7

Dusk settled along the empty stretch of road when Zeke finally called a halt to the day. Ahead of him the road disappeared into the river they'd been following.

"We can find a spot to spend the night over there by that bluff." He pointed to a solid rock wall away from the path.

Maeve barely nodded her head. She wasn't used to this kind of travel. Tomorrow night he'd put her up in a bed in the best hotel in town.

He dismounted, loosened the cinch, and let his horse drink its fill. The shuffle of feet and tired cadence of the mare had him sympathizing with the two females. He'd been a greenhorn once. The pace they'd kept since leaving Sumpter was close to a pony express rider's pace.

"Let me take care of your horse." He took the reins from her hands. "See if you can scrounge up some wood for a fire."

When she headed up river, he called to her,

"Don't go too far." The area was open, but the gulley and swales made it easy for someone to sneak up on them.

She nodded and began picking up drift wood along the river bank. He unsaddled the horses, made a fire pit, and gathered dead sagebrush and dry grass to start the fire. Smoke curled toward the sky, releasing the spicy sage tang into the air, as Maeve returned with an armload of wood.

Her nostrils flared. "What is that smell?"

"Haven't you ever smelled burning sagebrush?" This little whiff was nothing compared to the couple of range fires he'd encountered over the years.

"I guess not. It isn't the best smelling fuel for a fire."

"No, but it started the fire to warm our food and make a pot of coffee," he said, smiling and offering her a hand. He pulled her down beside him. "Sitting behind a desk and chasing rowdy boys isn't quite the same as putting miles under your horse."

"I can't remember when my body ached so much or I've felt so exhausted." She sat cross-legged with elbows resting on her knees, her hands propping up her head.

"Tomorrow night, you'll have a bed in a hotel. I promise." He grazed the side of her cheek with his knuckles. Why did this feisty woman bring out his protective nature? Most of the time she could take care of herself and him, but when she showed vulnerability he wanted to protect her.

"Between the hard ground and the saddle, my body feels bruised all over." She surprised him with a wisp of a smile. Then it disappeared, and he wanted to make it come back if even fleetingly.

"You could sleep on top of me," he offered, waggling his brows as he opened a can of beans.

"I don't believe you would be any softer than the ground."

Her retort shot his eyebrow up in question. "How could I not be softer than the ground?"

She blushed. The color darkened her cheeks as she licked her lips. Jacks and Jezebels. Her innocence when it came to men and women would be his undoing, he knew it as sure as he knew she would be his in the near future.

The splash of horses walking through water snapped his attention back to where it should have been. He placed the can of beans on a rock close to the fire and wiped his knife on his pant leg before slipping it into the boot sheath.

Maeve gasped and stiffened beside him. He placed a hand on hers. "Let's see who they are. Don't panic, I won't let anyone hurt you." He squeezed her hand and stood, waiting for the travelers to approach the fire.

Three horses and riders rode toward the fire. The sun had disappeared, but the moon cast a soft glow over the strangers. He sized up the intruders quickly. It was warm and dry enough to go without oilskins, yet they all wore them. The glint of metal escaped the opening of the leader's long coat.

Zeke stepped between Maeve and the riders. She grasped the back of his shirt and pulled herself to stand beside him.

"Mind if we share your fire?" the lead rider asked, leaning forward.

"We'll just pull our dinner. You're welcome to the fire," Zeke said, using a hand to move Maeve farther behind him.

The other two riders dismounted and started to lead their horses toward the mare and gelding.

"I'd prefer if you tied your horses over yonder," he said, pointing the opposite of where his horses grazed.

The mounted man nodded in that direction and stepped down off his horse. When the two walked by, he handed his reins to the closest man.

"You're not being all that hospitable," the man said, walking toward him.

Zeke extended his hand. "Just like to keep my stock away from other stock. Never know where or what they could have picked up. Especially if they do a lot of traveling."

The man ignored his offered hand and side-stepped to get a look at Maeve.

"I'd be hiding something that pretty, too." When the man reached out to touch her, Zeke slapped his arm away.

"Keep your hands to yourself, or I'll have to ask you to move on." He'd dropped his voice to a menacing growl and once again, used an arm to slide Maeve behind him.

The intruder was shorter and wiry. He had no doubt he could take the man, but he couldn't risk the others getting their hands on Maeve while he did.

The man raised his hands chest high and backed up, laughing. "Boys, guess we know where we stand with this filly."

The other men walked out of the shadows of

the bluff, laughing.

Zeke grasped Maeve's arm and walked her over to the saddles and horses.

"Stay here. I'm going to get the beans and coffee and come back. We'll eat and sleep over here." When she started to open her mouth, he put a finger on her lips. "I know this kind of man. It's best we stay our distance, but don't back down if they confront us."

He walked back to the fire. "We're done with the fire, it's all yours." Zeke picked up the beans and the coffee pot, moving back to the spot he left Maeve. He found the saddles, bedding and horses, but no woman.

The fool woman had to learn to follow orders. He refused to call to her and let the men know she wandered around alone. He glanced back at the fire. One of the men was missing.

A pile of boulders farther along the bluff was a likely spot to ambush a woman out wandering. He set the food on the ground away from the horse's feet and headed along the bluff, staying to the shadows. He rounded the first boulder.

A man had a hand over Maeve's mouth and one around her middle. He hauled his body back in an attempt to throw her to the ground like a calf about to be branded.

Zeke snuck up behind him and wrapped an arm around the assailant's neck, skillfully placing the point of his knife just below the man's jawbone.

"Let go of the woman or die."

Maeve fell to the ground when the man opened his arms. He started to struggle, and Zeke slit the skin along the man's jaw. Holding the knife blade down in the moonlight, the blood dripped onto the man's face.

"Go back to the fire, gather your friends and get out of here, or I'll slit all your throats." He shoved the man forward. When the coward took off running, he cleaned his knife and knelt over Maeve.

"Did he hurt you?" he asked, picking her up like a small child. Her arms slid around his neck, and she buried her face in his chest. Tears soaked his shirt as he carried her back to their horses.

He was relieved to see the men arguing. Maeve clung to him as he sat on a rock and watched the group. To his dismay they didn't saddle up. The leader walked over to them, his hand resting on the pistol revealed by his slung-back oilskin.

"I repeat, you ain't very hospitable." The man spat tobacco juice at Zeke's boot. Any other time, he'd have pounded the man's face, but he had the woman shivering in his arms to think about.

"You came to our fire. Then one of your men assaulted my wife." Maeve's head snapped up. He tucked it back under his chin. Now wasn't the time to let her little dislike of marriage surface. "I call that not being hospitable. Either get on your horses and ride out of here or get over by the fire and stay there." He glared at the man.

The leader looked from him to the shaking woman in his arms. After what seemed like hours, the man let his oilskin fall over his holster and walked back to the fire. But the group didn't leave. That was fine. He'd rather be able to keep an eye on them, then think they'd gone and have them double back and kill him and rape Maeve.

He pushed the loose strands of hair from her face and kissed her forehead. "Why did you leave without me?"

"I figured I could just slip behind the rocks and take care of some business." She hiccupped and ducked her head.

"No. Look at me." He held her head and made her look into his eyes. "All you had to do was tell me. I would have stood guard. There are times when you can't be so damned independent. And this was one of them."

She closed her eyes and nodded her head. He kissed her eyelids and waited for them to flutter open. "It looks like they aren't going to leave. So let's eat our dinner and then you lie down and sleep. I'll make sure they don't come near you."

Maeve sat up in his lap. "But you need sleep. We can take turns."

The smile that curved his lips, didn't light is eyes. She wondered if he would have killed the man had he done more than assaulted her. Fear prickled the hair on her head. Not of Zeke killing the man, but of what the man had attempted to do.

"No. You need your sleep. You aren't used to traveling. It's showing." His thumb touched her under the eye. "You've got circles."

He pulled the plates and cups out of the saddle bag and dished up their dinner. While she poured them each a cup of coffee, Zeke sliced the bread and watched the men laughing.

"They won't come over here will they?" she couldn't keep her voice from shaking.

"I don't know. The leader appears to have things handled, and I think he'll honor the fact I stood up to him." Zeke rubbed a hand over his face. "Kind of hard to see what he was really thinking with only the moonlight and his hat shading part of his face."

Maeve put her hand on his arm. "Thank you." Her fingers trembled, and she grasped his shirt. "I don't think I've ever been so scared. I'm also sorry I put you in that situation."

He placed his hand over hers. "This is all new. You'll learn to be more careful. And don't forget, you have that gun and a deadly aim. You don't have to be a victim."

She touched the pistol hanging at her side. The man had come up behind her so fast, she didn't have time to think, but the next time anyone tried it...

Zeke handed her a plate. They silently ate and watched the men growing louder at the fire. When they finished, they both walked down to the river and washed the dishes, then Zeke followed her to the boulders and stood guard while she finally had the chance to take care of business.

At the camp, Zeke rolled out both bedrolls side-by-side one against the wall of the bluff. "You crawl in the one to the back and cover up good. It's going to be cooler away from the fire."

Maeve started to protest, but he shook his head. He leaned against the bluff next to her, sharpening his knife and watching the men before he lay down with his back to her.

She tapped his shoulder.

"Yeah?"

"You need a blanket." She started to throw part of hers over him. His arm came up stopping the motion.

"I don't want to be wrapped up in a blanket if I have to move quick."

"Are you planning to stay awake all night?" she asked, wondering what use he would be for protection in the morning if he was too tired to stand.

"Only until they all fall asleep. Then I'll take a nap." He rolled to his back. His shoulder grazed her breast. The sensation made her body vibrate.

His gaze left the men and stared into her eyes. "If you aren't warm enough, just snuggle up to my back."

At the moment, she was more than warm enough. She nodded her head and pulled the blankets around her tighter. These feelings his touch evoked were new. She had no doubt, somewhere in her twenty-two years she'd missed out on some important information about what men could do to a woman's body.

She hadn't planned on snuggling against his back or falling asleep, but she did both and woke in the morning feeling refreshed.

Placing a hand on Zeke's shoulder, she peered over his sleeping form to catch a glimpse of their unwanted guests. The leader sat on the ground by the fire watching them. A shiver shuddered her body, and Zeke slid a hand back, drawing her tighter against him.

"I thought you were asleep," she said just above his ear as she continued to watch the man by the fire.

"I was until you touched me."

"I'm sorry." She ran her hand up and down his arm in a soothing motion.

"I'm not."

She heard the grin in his voice and smiled. The more she stuck around with him the more she felt herself uncoiling and enjoying life.

His hand squeezed the back of her thigh. Her heart beat rapidly, and the juncture between her legs pulsed. She gasped at the sensations.

Zeke flopped to his back, cupping her cheek in his large hand. "What's wrong?"

"N-nothing. I'm..." She pressed her face deeper into his palm, trying to snuff the heat in her cheeks.

"You're hot. Are you getting sick?" He sat up, pulling her up onto his lap.

She slapped at his arms and glanced over her shoulder. The man leered at them. "You're making a scene. One I don't want that man to see."

"You'd tell me if you were feeling puny, wouldn't you?" Zeke pressed his lips to her forehead then peered into her eyes.

"Yes, I'd let you know. I hate being sick. I'm not sick."

"Good. Let's just saddle up and get out of here. We'll nibble on some bread when we're farther away from those men."

She agreed with his idea. "Then unhand me, so I can stand and get busy." She grabbed his hat, plopping it on Zeke's head as he helped her stand. Again, his hands grasped her legs as she stood. The sensation wasn't as unsettling. His hands freely roaming her body with familiarity should have had her causing a scene. Instead, she welcomed his touch and realized she now knew the feelings of a woman.

The wide river had a broad bar of sandy soil with new grass in the middle. After trudging the horses through belly deep water, Zeke gave the animals a break on the built up silt and glanced back to make sure the riders remained at the camp. Satisfied they weren't followed, he urged his horse back into the river. The water on this side of the bar sloshed around the horse's knees. Once they were on solid ground, he kicked his gelding into a trot and Maeve followed. At this speed, they would be in The Dalles early enough to find the saloon, contact Barton, and still get cleaned up and enjoy a decent meal.

He'd spent most of the night watching the three men. They would have had to kill him to get their hands on Maeve. He wished he'd done more than scratch the one who had touched her. But he wouldn't have Maeve watch him kill a man. He wanted her to only see his gentle side, the one he projected when not helping his brother hunt down outlaws.

Zeke peered over his shoulder at the woman following him. He wasn't sure what he would do if they found out her father had made his living on the wrong side of the law. After his parents and brother were killed, he'd made a pact with himself to rid the world of murderers.

Maeve caught his gaze and held it. She was a child and had nothing to do with her father's indiscretions. Yet, he couldn't deny the coldness she was so adept at portraying. He'd learned it as an adult, but she clung to it like a person who'd lived with it her whole life.

She urged her horse up alongside. "When will we reach The Dalles?" The apprehension in her voice made him wonder if she knew something.

"We should be there mid-afternoon. Enough time to find Barton, clean up, have a good dinner, and get some decent sleep." He watched her hand flex at her hip. She was agitated. "What are you afraid we'll find?"

Her head jerked around, and her eyes narrowed. "I don't know what we'll find. My father alive and sorry he wrote that letter because it made me find him, or that he's been dead all these years and no one cared enough to tell us." A tear slid down her cheek. She swiped at it with a gloved hand and pushed her horse into a lope.

No matter how you looked at it, she had guts riding hell-bent toward devastating answers.

Chapter 8

Maeve couldn't ease the clench in her gut as the horses's hooves clomped on the packed dirt street of The Dalles. She'd never been to such a large town. At least not that she remembered. Buildings of varying sizes made out of wood, stone, and brick spread along the river and up the hill. The bustle around the train depot alone represented two days of activity in McEwen.

The street sported many saloons. She edged her horse closer to Zeke's as the traffic and people pressed around like an undertow of water. Most of the men and women wore city clothes, they looked proper. Rubbing her dirty leather gloves on her dusty riding skirt, she wanted to hide.

She hadn't dreamed The Dalles would be so large or urban. Tall stone buildings dwarfed smaller clapboard establishments. Her horse sidestepped a child running through the street. She couldn't look enough places at once. Her neck felt like the axle of a wheel as she whirled her head back and forth, watching the people and taking in the atmosphere.

Her horse stopped. Swinging her gaze to Zeke, she spotted the High Stakes Saloon in front of him. He dismounted and tied his horse to the rail. She couldn't move. Would the man who knew her father still be in this place?

"Come on, let's get this over with. I could use a bath and a good meal." Zeke reached up with both hands. His actions said more than words. He was there for her no matter what. She swung her leg over the horse's neck and slid down into his waiting arms.

At least she had his strength and compassion to cling to through this.

"Have you ever been in a saloon?" he asked, his hands still resting on her hips.

"No. But I've heard things." Things she didn't want to repeat. She glanced at the tall windows. The building was impressive. Respectable, even. However, as she stood conversing with Zeke, two men stumbled out the tall door, leaning heavily on one another.

"Stay close and act like you've been in this kind of place before. Wouldn't hurt to put a scowl on your face. Look like you're as tough as all those men in there put together." His lips curved in a mischievous grin, but his eyes remained hard.

"So in other words, act like we've just had a set-to."

"Yeah, only remember I'm your one ally in there." Zeke grabbed her hand and started to the building. At the door, he faced her, "And let me do the talking." He kissed her quick, dropped her hand, and shoved the door open.

Smoke hung in the rafters of the high ceiling. A polished bar stood along the back wall, the space in-between filled with tables, chairs, and men. Some dressed as though they'd been on the road like she and Zeke and others dressed like businessmen and bankers.

She followed Zeke's zigzag path through the tables to the bar. He stopped at the tall counter and surveyed the length of it. She took a spot next to him, following his lead of leaning one elbow on the counter, his body turned to keep an eye on the room.

A thin man, old enough to be her father, sporting a bushy, gray mustache, balding head, and an apron tied about his waist walked along the other side of the bar. He stopped across from them and sized Zeke up before smiling at her.

"What can I get you?" he asked, placing his hands on the shiny top and leaning her way.

She smiled at his disarming charm and waited for Zeke to say something.

"I'll have a beer." Zeke nodded toward her. "She'll have a sarsaparilla."

Maeve glared at Zeke. How was she supposed to appear tough if she drank sarsaparilla? "I'll have beer, too."

Zeke raised one eyebrow, but didn't say a word. The barkeep took two large mugs and filled them with an amber liquid. She ignored the apprehension bubbling in her belly and grabbed the handle when he placed a full beaker in front of her.

The crooked grin on Zeke's face as he raised his glass in a salute did nothing for her confidence.

She breathed in the scent of fermented grain and poured the warm liquid into her mouth. Bitterness assaulted her tongue before the beer slid down her throat and left the taste of sourdough starter in her mouth.

She wiped the foam off her upper lip with the sleeve of her blouse and smiled at Zeke. He set down his glass and cleared his throat.

"We're looking for a man named Barton."

She watched the barkeep. His welcoming smile became cautious and the friendly glow to his eyes faded.

"What do you want with him?" the man asked before he moved down the counter, taking money and handing out bottles and glasses. Zeke's eyes narrowed as his gaze followed the man.

"He knows him," she said, behind the mug as she took another sip.

"Yeah, he does." Zeke pushed her glass back down to the counter. "Don't drink too much. On an empty stomach it can make you do things you'll later regret."

"Really?" She studied the foam on the top of the drink. Did men drink on empty stomachs all the time? From the stories she'd heard, they all got drunk when they drank. She cast a sideways glance at Zeke. What would he be like drunk?

The man came back. "Who are you?"

"That depends on who you are and how we can get in touch with Barton." Zeke pushed his glass away and stared at the barkeep. This was Barton. He could feel it in the man's change of mood at the mention of the name.

"Ray, get over here!" the barkeep shouted to

a man who dealt cards at a nearby table. When the man moseyed over to the counter, the barkeep motioned for Zeke and Maeve to follow him to a table in a corner of the room. The man sat with his back in the corner, his guarded gaze watched the establishment.

Zeke took a chair to the side where he could also see the room and pulled Maeve down into a chair beside him.

The man leaned forward. His eyes appeared dark and hard as he stared at them. "I'll only ask this one more time. Who are you?"

"I'm Zeke Halsey." He nodded toward Maeve. "This is Maeve Loman."

The man's gaze darted to Maeve. He stared at her for a long time. "What do you want with Barton?"

"Her mother found a letter a while back, but just recently gave it to her. In it her father, Brendan Loman, told them to seek Barton at the High Stakes Saloon in The Dalles if he should not come home." Zeke studied the man who didn't take his gaze off Maeve. To her credit, she stared right back at him, never flinching.

"He didn't come home ten years ago."

The barkeep's head snapped up to look at Zeke. "Ten years? And you're just now looking for me?"

His instincts were right. This was Barton. "Maeve's mother was a little—"

"Distraught over my father not returning. And she didn't find the letter until she moved to Baker City with my aunt." Maeve cut in.

"Why did she show it to you now? I would

have thought she'd been anxious about her husband?" Barton watched Maeve. He knew something about Mrs. Loman. Zeke could see it in the vein pulsing on the man's temple.

"It's a long story," Zeke started, "my brother's wife found a tintype in a cabin where some outlaws were holed up." Barton seemed to perk up. "The tintype was of my parents who were killed by Indian's years ago. At least we thought so until this tintype surfaced."

Barton leaned back in his chair, studying him. Did he see a light of recognition in the man's dark eyes?

"Anyway, I showed the tintype to Maeve since I plan to marry her." The woman next to him cleared her throat. He put a hand over hers and continued. "She said it was a picture of her uncle. That her pa had said the man in the tintype was his brother."

A mirthless grin stretched across Barton's lips, and his head nodded slightly.

"Seeing as how we want to get married," he felt her tug on the hand under his, "we wanted to make sure we weren't related. Maeve's ma said they weren't blood kin, but they knew each other during the war."

Barton nodded his head. Not a good sign. Zeke was positive there was no way his pa could have been anywhere near the war.

"And that's when she gave Maeve the letter from her pa—unopened." He studied the man. Barton knew about Mr. Loman and his pa. His gut tightened. Something in his father's past wasn't going to set well. He could feel it in the calculating stare and mirthless smile of the man sitting at the table glancing back and forth between him and Maeve.

"I can set your minds at rest about being blood kin. You're not," Barton said, as though he were a preacher redeeming them.

He'd believed that all along, but hearing it was a relief. He rubbed his thumb back and forth across Maeve's hand. Tremors echoed into his palm. Glancing into her eyes, he was relieved to see the statement didn't bother her. They'd become closer on this journey. He'd hate to see her push him away.

"As to your father's demise," Barton peered at Maeve, "all I can say is, I thought he'd finished a job and finally went home to stay."

"W-what do you mean a job?" Maeve turned her hand palm up and clutched Zeke's hand.

"What do you know about your pa?" Barton asked, lowering his voice and settling his forearms on the table, leaning toward them.

Maeve leaned in. "He left my mother and I a great deal—to hunt for gold. And he worked as a freighter for a while."

Barton rubbed a hand over his face and tugged on the end of his mustache. "He never went after gold, but he did work as a freighter before he fell in with some despicable people."

Fear gripped her chest. Had he been an outlaw? If so, did she really want to find out what happened to him? For all she knew he could have been hanged.

"You're not telling us everything." The flat, low tone of Zeke's voice reflected his feelings toward her father. She tried to pull her hand from his, but he clasped it harder.

"I can't tell you any more here. And it isn't a good idea if people find out who you are," his gaze flickered to Maeve, "or you to be seen talking to me."

She leaned away from the man. Was he just as despicable as her father? How were they to trust his answers?

"We're going to get a room, a bath, and dinner. Is there some place we can meet you after that and talk?" Zeke stiffened when a group of men entered the establishment.

Her gaze drifted to the door, and her head throbbed. It was the men from the night before. Why had they followed them? The group had been headed the opposite direction last night.

"You know them?" Barton asked, scowling.

"Only in passing. They invaded our camp last night." Zeke glared at the group.

Maeve didn't want to look at them. She stared at Zeke and felt his anger as he gripped her hand.

"This might work to your favor. Watch your back with those men, but they will lead you to the truth about Loman." Barton stood. "I'll send a messenger to the Umatilla House with where to meet me."

When Zeke finally looked at him, he added, "It's the best place in town, has all the amenities you just listed. When you sign in, do it as Mr. and Mrs. You don't want anyone to know you're related to Loman."

"But..." She started to go after the man. Zeke's tight grip on her hand stopped her.

"Don't make a scene." He let go of her hand and pressed his palm against her back, moving her toward the door.

She started to turn around to protest, however, the look on his face made her swing back around and march to the door. Once they were outside, she faced him.

"We can't sign in as husband and wife. That means—" she felt her cheeks heat. "That means we'll be sharing a room."

"What sleeping next to me under the stars is better than in a room?" The smile on his face didn't light up his eyes. His attention was focused on the man exiting the building.

She shivered. It was the man who accosted her the night before.

"Come on." Zeke untied her horse and lifted her onto the saddle before swinging up on the back of his gelding. He started down the street, and she followed not wanting to be left behind for that man to grab her again.

She glanced over her shoulder.

The man stared right back at her, leering.

Maybe pretending to be married to Zeke wasn't such a bad idea.

Chapter 9

"I'll get you settled in a room and take the horses to the livery," Zeke said, pulling the bedroll and saddlebag from his horse.

Maeve stared at the three-story-high, huge, square building. A balcony ran around the second story. It was the biggest building she'd ever laid eyes on. When she stood staring, Zeke came around and gathered her bedroll and saddlebag.

"You never see a building before," he asked, taking her by the elbow and heading for the entrance.

"Not one this big." They stepped through the doors and she stopped. "Or this fancy."

Zeke escorted her to a large, ornately carved counter. In the middle of the lobby sat a wood stove with several men in chairs chatting. They stopped long enough to rake a look at the pair, before talking again.

The man behind the counter smiled congenially. "Welcome to Umatilla House."

"Thanks. My wife and I'd like a room on the second floor." Zeke signed the large book on the counter. The way he said 'my wife' hummed in Maeve's heart even as it frustrated her. She wasn't happy with pretending to be married or sharing a room with him. And why was Barton worried about people knowing her name? Was her father so despicable they would turn on her? She shuddered at the thought.

The man read the name in the book and smiled. "Mr. and Mrs. Halsey, I hope you enjoy your stay." He handed Zeke a key. "You'll have room two-ten."

"Thank you." Zeke started to move away from the counter then turned back. "Could you have a tub and water brought up?"

"I'll send someone right up with water and a tub." The man slapped his hand on a bell and an adolescent young man appeared from the back room.

Zeke grasped her elbow and headed up the stairs. The carpeted steps muffled their boot heels as they climbed to the second floor. A bath sounded lovely. But she wouldn't disrobe or step in a tub if he remained in the room. It would be inappropriate. His dark eyes watching— her body warmed at the thought.

Shiny, brass kerosene lamps lit the carpeted hallway.

At room two-ten, Zeke opened the door and gestured for her to go ahead of him. It was a large room with a tall feather bed placed in the corner. A nightstand stood on one side with a brass kerosene lamp. A matching pitcher and bowl sat on a fancy carved wash stand next to a wood stove with a boiler reservoir.

Zeke crossed the room, dropping the saddlebags on the two upholstered chairs next to a small table beside the window. When he drew back the curtain, she caught a glimpse of the river.

"Take your hat and gloves off and get comfortable," he said, leaning against the end of the bed and watching her.

"What about you? And this bath? I'll not have you in the room while I'm bathing." Her stomach fluttered when his eyes lit with desire.

"I'm only staying until they get the tub here and it's filled." He stepped in front of her and unbuckled her holster, looping it over the bedpost. His gaze drifted over her face, then peered into her eyes as he pulled her hat from her head and finger by finger removed her gloves. The slow movements and intent look elicited a tingle down her spine.

"Excuse me," muttered a red-faced, young man at the door. "The tub."

She jumped and Zeke moved around her to help the young man set the tub in a spot which appeared to be reserved for that purpose. The boy opened the door on the stove and knelt in front of it, lighting the already waiting kindling. When the sticks popped and hissed, he stood.

"I'll be back with the water," his voice cracked. He kept his eyes averted before he darted out, leaving the door gaping.

She giggled. The boy obviously thought he'd interrupted something. She glanced at Zeke. He stalked across the room, pulling her into his arms. His lips descended upon hers before she could think of resisting.

The slow seduction of his mouth weakened her knees. He caught her in his arms, carrying her to one of the chairs. Zeke sat, cradling her on his lap. She closed her eyes as his soft lips dropped kisses down her jawline. Tilting her head back, she allowed access to his talented lips which continued on a path down her neck to the buttons on her blouse.

Heat curled in her lower regions. Her breasts felt full and ached. She wound her hands in his hair, knocking his hat to the floor and brought his lips back to hers. When a sigh escaped her parted lips, his tongue entered and seduced her even more.

A knock on the open door and Zeke's body jerking, brought her back to reality. He set her on the chair as he stood. She noticed he walked a little stiff, like most mornings after he'd slept next to her. The face on the boy standing at the open door was as red as the long john's she'd seen hanging on clothes lines on laundry day.

And he wasn't alone. A China man stood behind him with full buckets. She stared out the window barely seeing the river as mortification engulfed her. Those males had seen her being eaten alive by Zeke. And it didn't help they all thought they were married. Even married people didn't act that way in front of others. At least none of the married people she'd ever been around.

When the buckets had been dumped and one sat next to the stove to replenish the reservoir, Zeke closed the door. He ran a hand through his already mused hair and looked at her like a boy who'd just dipped a braid in the inkwell.

"I'm sorry. I didn't think about the door being open and—well so many people seeing—you know."

"See it doesn't happen again." She turned her attention back to the rapidly moving water in the river below. She'd enjoyed the kisses. That was part of the problem. Her emotions had to be held back until they knew more about her father.

"I don't think I can."

She wrenched her head around and found Zeke standing beside the chair. "Can't what?"

"Keep my hands off you. But I won't compromise you. I promised. I keep my promises." Zeke leaned down. She waited for him to place a kiss on her cheek, but he picked up his hat and straightened.

"You think pretending to be married isn't compromising me?" This was what she needed. A good argument to put him at a distance.

"We're pretending to be married to keep you safe." He placed his hands on his hips and stared at her like she was a daft child.

"Safe from what? What could my father have done that ten years later his name would cause me harm?" She stared into his cold, unflinching gaze. A slight movement caught her eye. The muscle in his jaw twitched. What had turned him from ardent to agitated? The hardness in his eyes unsettled her in a different way than his kisses.

"We won't know until we find out. Take a bath." Zeke crossed to the door. With his hand on the cut-glass knob, he turned back to her. "Lock this behind me and keep your gun close."

He slipped out the door, and she hurried to

lock it behind him. With trembling fingers she hung her holster on the peg on the wall above the tub.

She dipped her hand in the steaming liquid and sighed. The velvety water caressed her fingers.

Dropping her dirty clothes to the floor, she slid into the warm, inviting tub. Being dirty while traveling hadn't bothered her, but being in town, she wanted to look respectable. Or as respectable as she could in a riding skirt.

Zeke noticed the man who'd accosted Maeve sitting in the corner of the lobby. Why did he watch them? And why had those men changed their direction, returning to The Dalles? He didn't like all these questions and even less the thought Maeve was in danger from a father that hadn't been in her life for a decade.

Frowning, he went out to the horses and wasn't a bit surprised when the man followed him. At least if the man dogged him, he wouldn't have time to report Maeve was at the Umatilla alone.

He mounted his horse and led the mare down to the livery they'd passed earlier. On the way, he noticed a dress shop and on the other side of the livery was a sign for baths. He handed the horses over to the stable boy and paid for several days. There was no telling how long they'd have to stay to find out about Loman.

Backtracking through town, he found a store that sold men's clothing and purchased a white shirt, riding trousers, drawers, and a brown, corduroy vest. He hurried back to the bath house with his purchases. The older woman running the place could have been his grandmother. Her smile showed tobacco-stained teeth, and the faded brown eyes sized him up as he walked through the door.

"You looking to clean up?" she asked, as her gaze slid down his body and back up to his face. "For an extra coin you can get your back washed." The grandmother winked and a scantily dressed woman Maeve's age stepped from behind a curtained partition.

"I just need a bath ma'am." When the girl pouted he added, "Nothing against you," he smiled, "I'm married."

"That hasn't stopped many men before," the old woman said, handing him a towel. "Third room on the left."

Zeke touched the brim of his hat and headed down the hall. Saying he was married was a whole lot better than telling them he only wanted one woman in a tub of water with him. And she was sitting in her own bath back at the Umatilla.

He pushed aside the canvas covering the third door and stepped into a room with a large, wooden tub. He undressed and climbed in. The water was tepid, but not for long. The young woman, who offered to wash his back, lugged in two steaming buckets of water. Zeke grabbed his hat, holding it over his crotch as the woman smiled and emptied the buckets near his feet.

"You sure you don't want me to at least wash your hair?" She leaned forward giving him a clear view of her ample breasts. They were a sight, but not the ones he wanted to see.

"Sorry, I can take care of myself." He shot her

a smile, but she huffed out of the room, flinging the canvas shut behind her.

After scrubbing, shaving, and donning the new clothes, Zeke rolled his dirty clothes up in the paper the new clothes had been wrapped in and wandered back out to the main room. The old woman raised an eyebrow. He'd been told on more than one occasion he cleaned up well.

"Your wife is one lucky woman," the old lady said, leaning on the counter, resting her abundant breasts on the smooth wood.

"I'm the lucky one," he said, walking up to the counter. "Have you been around here a long time?"

"Since the first load of miners came through in a huff to make their fortunes." The woman scoffed and pulled a half-chewed cigar from under the counter.

"A friend of my father's was here about ten years ago. He might have used your facilities." The woman nodded for him to divulge the name. Zeke hesitated. Would he put them in more danger by asking questions? The name had to come out to get anywhere.

Leaning close, he said, "His name was Brendan Loman. You know him?"

Her eyes widened, and she chomped down on the cigar before narrowing her eyes and jabbing a finger at him. "You might want to watch who you tell that to."

"Why? What did he do?" Zeke felt his jaw clenching and slowly worked it loose. His anger at anyone who worked outside the law always set him off.

"Not so much what he did, it's what others

thought of what he did." She looked around and lowered her voice. "It's best you don't mention that name too loud around the gaming establishments. There's a lot of bitterness."

Someone entered the door. She straightened and pasted a smile on her face. "You and your wife have a nice stop over," she said, clearly indicating it wasn't a good idea to hang around.

Zeke turned and nearly bumped into the man who'd accosted Maeve. He put his hand in the middle of the man's chest and shoved him back against the wall. "When I told you to stay away from my wife I meant it." He wanted to pound the statement into the man, but couldn't take the chance he'd end up in jail, leaving Maeve unprotected.

He exited the establishment and shook his shoulders. It took years after his parent's death to learn to control his short fuse. Since the discovery of Maeve's past, he'd been holding it on a tight rein. Lowlifes like the men following him, rankled. There was a reason they followed. And it couldn't be good.

Tucking his dirty clothes under his arm, Zeke set off for the dress shop he'd seen. There was a way to make up to Maeve for compromising her.

Chapter 10

Maeve sat in a chair staring out the window wondering when Zeke would return. Her stomach had started rumbling when she dressed. She ran her hands down the sides of the extra riding skirt she'd packed. If she'd known they would be in such a large city she would have packed a day dress at least.

A knock at the door startled her. She picked up her gun from the table in front of her and crossed the room.

She cocked the pistol. "Who's there?"

"Zeke."

She opened the door to the familiar voice, but just about shut it again at the pile of packages covering the person. She recognized the dusty Stetson above the parcels, as belonging to the man who brought her to town.

She stepped back. Zeke entered and dumped the packages on the bed.

"Keep the door closed." He strode back to the

door, closing it and turning the key in the lock.

Frowning, she glanced from the pile of packages to the man, standing cross-armed and looking quite dapper, studying her.

"What are all of these for?" She waved a hand toward the brown paper-wrapped items.

"You. I can't take you to a fancy restaurant looking like some outlaw in that riding skirt." He smiled and her heart fluttered. Gone were the dark whiskers that had shaded his features since leaving Sumpter. His handsome face appeared smooth. Breathing deeply, she inhaled the masculine scent of bay rum.

"You don't have to take me to a fancy restaurant." She stepped to the bed and picked up the largest package. Before she turned it over in her hands, Zeke stood beside her and ripped the paper.

"We've been invited to a fancy restaurant by Barton." Zeke's voice held a tinge of suspicion.

"You don't trust him?" She scanned his set jaw and narrowed eyes.

"It just seems strange he didn't want to talk to us at the saloon, but he's willing to dine out in a public restaurant with us—It just doesn't add up is all." He pulled a dark green dress out of the paper.

She ran her hand over the finely woven fabric. "This is—"

"You like it?" Zeke held the dress up in front of her.

"It's beautiful, but you shouldn't have spent your money on it. On me." Raising her face, she gazed into his eyes. It pleased him to do this. She saw it in the crinkles by his eyes and the way the dark orbs lit up. But to take clothing, especially such expensive ones from him, would give him thoughts of a future with her. That was something she couldn't risk. Not yet. Not when her father's past could make Zeke think less of her than he did at this moment. And what if they found her father? Her mother constantly told her she was just like him.

"We have to meet Barton. I figured you didn't bring any fancy clothes in that saddlebag." He kicked the empty saddlebag on the floor beside the bed. "Take this, and know I don't want anything from you for having the pleasure of dressing you up."

She searched his eyes. Sincerity glistened. With a nod, she accepted the dress, hoping he meant what he said—he didn't expect anything. The fineness of the garment and the color took her breath away. She'd never owned anything so grand. Her clothes had always been serviceable. She never wore anything that would attract a man's attention.

Gazing up at Zeke, she knew his eyes wouldn't leave her all night, and not because she could be in danger. Her insides jiggled.

"Open the other packages and make sure I didn't forget anything." He pushed the smaller packages toward her.

It was like Christmas, only better, because it was so unexpected. She unwrapped drawers, an underskirt, and a camisole with lace edging, stockings, and soft, satin slippers in a color that matched the dress.

"How did you know to get all of this?" Maeve stared at the garments scattered across the bed.

"The woman in the store helped." He grasped her shoulders and turned her to him. "Do you like it?"

"It's all wonderful." Tears burned her eyes. She didn't want him to see how his thoughtfulness touched her. No one had ever presented her with so much. Pushing him toward the door, she said, "You'll have to leave so I can change."

"How long will it take?" The eager look on his face let her know he was anxious to strut about town with her on his arm.

"Thirty minutes. Now go."

"Lock this behind me."

She scooped the dress from the bed as the door clicked shut. Hurrying across the room, she snapped the key to lock the door and danced back to the bed with the garment in her arms.

Zeke walked into the Umatilla Saloon and immediately felt the charge of the gamblers gathered around tables scattered throughout the room. It was late afternoon, yet the place did a brisk business not only in gambling but drinking and socializing.

He'd barely scanned the room when he spotted the three men following them. He itched to know who they were but refrained from walking up and asking. Standing at the bar where he could watch them, he struck up a conversation with the old timer next to him.

"You don't happen to know those three sitting at the table in the far corner?" he asked, flagging the barkeep down and ordering the man another finger of whiskey.

"What'cha want to know for?" The old timer took a swallow from his glass.

"The one looks like a man who knew my father. I don't like making a fool of myself." He took a sip of whiskey. Not knowing where Maeve stood on a man getting drunk, he'd have to stay sober to keep his promise and not compromise her later tonight when they slept in the same room. He winced at the thought of her sleeping in the bed while he slept on the hard floor.

The old man tossed back the glass, dribbling the amber liquid down his chin, and looked at the three in the corner. "The oldest one is Jack Marsh. His brother was murdered 'bout ten years ago. He's been a bit tetched since. The other two follow him like besotted ugly women. Don't have a good head between 'em."

Zeke watched the leader in the mirror behind the bar. "Guess he isn't who I thought he was."

The old man grunted and studied his glass.

Now he had a name to ask Barton about. The timing was right, but why did the men follow them? That didn't make sense. There was no way he could know Maeve was related to Loman.

He nursed his drink watching the men and the gamblers engrossed in their games. A large man at a corner table roared loudly and slapped the winnings in the middle of the table. Those losing their money didn't seem the least bit upset to lose to the jovial man.

When the barkeep came back to replenish his glass, Zeke asked, "Who's the man at the corner table?"

The barkeep smiled. "That's Hardley, one of the owners. He likes to mingle with the customers. Sinnott is the man at the front desk. He enjoys meeting the patrons."

He nodded and slipped his watch out of his pocket. Thirty minutes. That was all he would give Maeve. He was hungry for food and to feast his eyes on her in that dress.

Maeve paced the floor. Her hair was piled on her head with tendrils tickling her neck. Everything fit perfectly. She had only one problem. The dress buttoned up the back. No matter how she twisted, she couldn't slip a button through a hole.

A knock startled her from her reveries on how to finish the task.

"Maeve, it's me, Zeke." He rattled the knob, and she stopped squirming as her feet rooted to the middle of the room.

The man who'd begun to trickle into her heart stood on the other side of the door. He was also the only person she knew who could button her dress.

"Maeve?" The slight rise of his worried voice put her feet into motion. She crossed the room and flicked the key.

The door opened so fast she jumped backward. Zeke wrapped his arms around her, embracing her to his hard chest.

"When you didn't answer the door, I thought..." His body shook. Before she could soak up his worry, he held her out in front of him. "What's wrong?"

She felt small for having given him such concern, but now he was in the room, her face heated.

"Maeve?" He placed a warm finger under her chin, tipping her face to look up into his.

"I-I-" she turned her back to him. She couldn't ask him to button her dress and look at him.

The deep chuckle rumbled behind her and sent her embarrassment flying. How dare he find humor in her situation. His knuckles brushed her skin, and she forgot her anger. The sensation of his rough skin against hers sent shivers gliding up her back.

"Sorry, when the lady at the store showed me this dress I just thought the color would look good, I never thought about how you'd get into it." The sincerity in his voice made her look over her shoulder at him.

Their gazes locked, his hands stilled. She wanted to repay him for all his kindness—that was all. Lifting an arm, she grasped his neck, pulling his head down. Before she lost her nerve, she placed her lips on his.

Zeke groaned and spun her in his arms, drawing her tight against him and deepening the kiss. His rough hands branded her skin through the flimsy chemise when they slid through the open back of her dress. His mouth did wondrous things to her lips. When she opened, his entrance stoked a fire within. Her body came alive, pressing against him. The evidence of his arousal no longer scared her.

In fact, she'd become curious. Pushing her body tighter against his, she felt the length of his hardness against her stomach.

Zeke pushed away from her groaning. He

stood with his back to her.

"I'm sorry. I won't do that again," she said appalled at being so forward. How could she have let her curiosity and his kisses make her think she could touch a man in such a way?

"Honey, after we're married you can press against me all you want. Until then..." Zeke faced her as he raked a hand through his hair and willed his hardness to subside. Her body pressed to his had just about caused him to let loose. He'd been so scared someone had taken her when she didn't answer the door right away he'd let things get out of hand.

Roughly he spun her around and finished buttoning the damn dress. Why had he bought one with so many buttons? And up the back where she couldn't do it herself. He let out a breath.

It wasn't her fault. He was always pushing her to make a move like she just did. Only he wouldn't take her to bed until she agreed to marry him. He cared for her too much to ruin her chances at happiness with someone else. The thought didn't sit well in his gut, but if when this ordeal was over, she still didn't believe he would stick with her no matter what—he'd leave her alone.

"There. You're all trussed up and I'm starving." He picked his hat up off the floor before glancing at her. Despite her flushed face, a polite smile tipped the corners of her mouth. The loose tendrils of hair trailing down her neck made him salivate. She had the look of a woman ready to be seduced.

"I'm hungry, too," she said, plucking her holster from the bedpost.

"Nope. That stays here. You aren't going to

ruin your pretty appearance by hanging that thing from your hip." He grabbed the holster and gun, thrusting them under the mattress. "It'll be there when we return."

He extended an arm and escorted her down the stairs. The appreciative stares from the men in the lobby puffed his chest and made him place a possessive hand over Maeve's hand on the crook of his arm.

"Are we walking?" Maeve asked her voice barely above a whisper.

"Yes." He smiled and led her into the large, opulent dining room of the Umatilla.

"Oh! I've never seen anything like it!" The woman by his side stared in awe at the large, richly decorated walls and expansive, dark wood furniture.

"I can seat you," offered a finely-dressed man sporting a mustache and dutiful smile.

"Thank you. We'll have someone joining us shortly." Zeke took Maeve by the hand. He loved the contact of her skin against his. She smiled and squeezed his hand as they followed the waiter. Again, he pondered the change in her. Even though they still didn't know what lurked in her father's past, she'd smiled at him more in the last two days than the whole year he'd spent courting her.

When the waiter stopped, Zeke positioned the table at an angle so they could sit watching the entrance to the room. He held a chair for Maeve and she sat. Hovering over her gave him an excellent view of the creamy swells holding up her lacy neckline.

The waiter cleared his throat and motioned for

him to sit. He pulled his pocket watch out before sitting in the chair next to Maeve. They were early, but he was starving, and he'd heard Maeve's stomach rumble as they walked down the stairs.

"We won't wait for the other person. Bring us two specials with coffee." He glanced at Maeve to see if his order pleased her. She nodded.

When the waiter walked away, he leaned close. "When Barton gets here, let's see what he says before saying anything."

Maeve stiffened. He glanced toward the door. Damn. Marsh and his two idiots stood inside the doorway. The leader scanned the room and smiled when he sighted Maeve. Why were they following? He looked at the woman beside him. Had she said something to the man who accosted her?

He took her hand in both his. She trembled. "Maeve, look at me."

Watching the men scared her, yet she seemed to be reluctant to take her gaze from them.

"I don't understand why those men are following us." He took a deep breath and spit out the words. "Did you say anything to the man that accosted you?"

Her head jerked around. She pulled on the hand clasped in his. "No!" Her voice was harsh and bitter. She shot to her feet, but he pulled her back down onto the chair.

"I'm not insinuating anything. I know you didn't do anything to attract that man, but you never told me the details." He brushed a wisp of hair back, skimming her cheek with his knuckles. "Did he start a conversation or just grab you?"

A wave of revulsion shook her body. Maeve

saw the concern and censure in Zeke's eyes. She knew he had a reason for his question. She'd put the event out of her mind until the man showed up in The Dalles. Now he and his attack plagued her like an abscess.

"I never had a chance to say anything. He snuck up behind me as I was—" she gulped. The repulsive man had hooked an arm around her waist as she started to unbutton her skirt preparing to relieve herself.

"Shh." Zeke raised her hand to his lips. "I didn't bring it up to upset you. I'm trying to figure out why they followed us."

Maeve nodded. The man holding her hand would never hurt her. Not intentionally anyway.

"I learned today the leader is Jack Marsh. His brother was killed ten years ago."

She snapped to attention. Ten years ago. When her father went missing. "Do you think?"

"That's one of the questions I plan to put to Barton."

The waiter arrived with their food. Before the man could back away, they both started eating. She was the first to shove her plate to the middle of the table and relax against the chair back.

She sighed. Living on trail rations the last few days had given her a new appreciation for food.

Zeke flipped his pocket watch open and frowned. "Barton's late."

She glanced to the entry. .

"Damn!" Zeke stared at the empty corner table where the three men had sat. "Come on." He tossed gold coins on the table and grasped her hand, pulling Maeve to her feet.

Chapter 11

"Where are we going?" Maeve held the skirt of her dress in her free hand as she hurried behind Zeke's long strides.

"To change." He pulled her up the stairs to the second floor and wrenched the door open.

"But..."

He closed the door, locked it, and spun her around. His touch singed her skin as he quickly unfastened her buttons.

"Get into your riding skirt. We're going to go find Barton." He snatched his saddlebag from the arm of a chair and turned with his back facing her.

She marched to the bed, wishing she could climb into it and sleep until noon the next day. The sound of Zeke changing his clothes pushed her into motion. She didn't want him to turn around before she'd dressed.

Shoving the dress down her body, she plucked a blouse from her open saddle bag and buttoned it quickly. She'd leave the fancy undergarments on. There was no way she'd strip to her skin with him in the room. Her face heated, and her fingers trembled as she untied the strings on her petticoats, dropping them to the floor in a white mound over the dress. Standing in a blouse and her drawers, she quickly grabbed the riding skirt thrown across the end of the bed.

"You done?" Zeke's deep voice caused her to jump.

"Almost." She stepped into her riding skirt and buttoned the waist. "Now."

He strode across the room and looked down at her feet. "Change out of those shoes."

She kicked off the fancy shoes and stepped into her boots. Zeke knelt in front of her and fastened her boots.

"Leave your clothes on the bed. I paid for the room for several days, so things should be here when we get back." He raised the mattress and handed Maeve her gun and holster.

She buckled the holster, settled it on her hips, and grabbed her hat as Zeke grasped her hand, dragging her to the door.

"What's the hurry?" she asked as he took the key from the door and locked it from the outside once they stood in the hall.

"If Barton's running, we need to get on his trail." He took her hand, leading her down the hall to the back of the building.

"If?"

"Those three disappeared from the restaurant."

She shivered. "You think they might have done something to Barton?"

"I don't know. But the first place we're headed

is the High Stakes." Their boots tapped a staccato beat down the back stairs.

Zeke's large hand was warm and comforting as they plunged into the shadows behind the buildings. She caught a shimmer of moonlight on the wide river before he drew her down a dark alley. Maeve hurried her steps to keep close to Zeke. The piles of boxes a ruffian could hide behind moved her legs even faster.

Out on the street, kerosene lanterns illuminated the board walkways and dirt road. "This way." He squeezed her hand and continued to his left. He veered to the right at the corner. The noisy street startled her. Men and horses milled about with regard to no one. Piano music floated out of the saloons, mingling and becoming an odd background for the shouting and fist fights in the street.

She pushed against Zeke unable to believe men behaved this way. They were no different than a bunch of rowdy school boys. Zeke pulled her into his arms when a large man stumbled into the street. The stranger's hand latched onto her pistol when he attempted a grab at her.

Instinct brought her knee up to collide with the man's crotch. He howled in pain, clutching the juncture of his legs with both hands. She felt the weight of her gun back in her holster. Placing a hand over it, she continued to the saloon, tucked against Zeke.

"Nice job," he complimented, pushing the door open for her to enter the High Stakes saloon. "I'm never going to try and take your gun." The mischief glinting in his eyes made her smile.

Acrid smoke and unwashed bodies wrinkled

her nose. A wide, firm hand on her back propelled her through the tables crowded with men. The clink of glass and chink of coins rang out above the rumble of male voices.

Zeke pushed her up to the bar. His arms latched onto the counter on either side of her providing a barrier between herself and the men along the counter. When the barkeep approached, she smiled, hoping that was what he expected.

"Where's Barton?" Zeke's voice roared over her shoulder. The man shrugged and held up an empty glass.

"You here to drink or talk? I ain't got time for talking." The barkeep filled the glass and handed it to someone to the right of them.

Zeke studied the man as he digested the information. The curve of Maeve's backside pushed against his groin, made it hard to remember why he was in the bar. He focused on the man behind the counter. "Barton was supposed to meet us and didn't show."

"He asked me to work tonight because he had something to do." The barkeep looked them over. "But he was dressed too fancy to be meeting the likes of you."

Maeve's body stiffened against his chest. Probably ready to give the man a tongue lashing.

"Does he live above the saloon?"

"Yeah, but you won't find him there. I seen him walk out the door myself."

Maeve spun in front of him. Her breasts pushed against his chest. He didn't know which was more distressing—her backside or her front side rubbing against him.

"Come on." He hooked his arm in hers and headed to the back of the room.

"Where are we going?"

He noticed she kept a hand over her pistol. She was a quick learner. "We're going to have a look at Barton's room."

"You know which one it is?"

"No, but we'll figure it out."

They stepped out the back entrance and moved to the stairs leading to the upper level.

She stopped, pulling her arm out of his. "If you don't know which room is Barton's, how do you expect to learn anything?"

"I think, since he was all dressed up, he had planned to meet us. Something happened." He started up the stairs, hoping she followed.

She did. "But if he was dressed up and headed to the Umatilla, he didn't make it. What good is it going to do to look in his room? Obviously something happened between here and the restaurant."

He turned the knob on the door and entered a hallway. It was dark, but by the moonlight streaming through the open door, he could see three doors on the hallway. Being a betting man, he figured the lone door on the one side of the hall would be the room belonging to the man who owned the establishment.

The soft footfalls of Maeve as she followed him to the door reassured him she hadn't stood out on the landing in plain sight.

He tried the knob. It didn't turn. He pulled out his knife and ran it between the door and the jamb, popping the door loose.

"I've never seen that done before." The wonder

and not criticism in her voice surprised him. He'd expected a lecture on the proprieties of breaking into someone's room.

"It's not something I do on a regular basis. Only in emergencies." He slid his knife back in the boot sheath and stepped into the room. Maeve was already flitting about.

"There's nothing here." She stood in the room her arms spread like a bird about to take flight.

"We haven't looked yet." He debated if he should light a lantern and risk being found.

"There's nothing to look for." She pushed the curtains back on the one window, allowing more light to enter the room.

She was right. The room had the appearance of a hotel room. There was nothing personal in plain sight. No trunk, no tintypes, not even a book. He opened the drawers on a chest and found basic clothing items. A razor, strap, and shave soap along with a comb were tucked into the top drawer. That was as close to personal belongings he could find.

"This is sad." Maeve's voice wavered.

"Why?"

"How old do you think Barton is? Fifty? And he has nothing. This room shows me a man who is lonely. He has no family and apparently no interest in women or a wife." She crossed her arms. "That's the saddest thing I've ever seen."

Hope swelled in his chest. This was the first time she'd voiced thoughts of having a family.

He stepped beside her, gathering her into an embrace. Her head rested against his chest. He breathed in the scent of freshly washed hair and floral skin. He'd give anything to be able to place her on the bed and show her she would never be alone as long as he lived.

She wiped at her eyes. "So now what do we do?"

"Find out where Jack Marsh and his friends hole up." Her body stiffened in his arms, but she nodded her head. "Don't worry. I won't let anyone hurt you."

She brushed a wisp of hair off his forehead. "I know."

He resisted the urge to kiss her, knowing once he started, he'd lose sight of what they had to do. Instead, he gave her a brief hug and captured her hand.

"Let's go back to the Umatilla and see if we can learn more about Jack Marsh."

Several hours later, Maeve followed Zeke down the street to the livery. It had taken two bottles of whiskey for the old man and two beers for she and Zeke to get the codger to tell them everything he knew about Marsh. If it hadn't been for the holes under the counter she slid her fingers into for support, she would have never been able to keep from falling down as Zeke finally cajoled the information out of the old man.

Her head felt fuzzy. She tried hard to remember if the old codger mentioned the name of the man who'd killed Marsh's brother. Surely, her beer-saturated brain would have picked up on her father's name had it been mentioned.

While Zeke saddled the horses, she wandered out behind the building to find a privy. Her head buzzed, and her body didn't quite respond to what she wanted it to do. She found the privy, stepped inside, and sat. The small building closed in around her. Warm, putrid air convulsed her stomach; she closed her eyes against the swaying door. Closing her eyes didn't help. She leaned her head against the side of the structure to stop it from moving.

The horses were saddled. Zeke looked around.

Where'd Maeve go? She knew better than to wander around this town unescorted.

"You see the woman I came in here with?" he asked the boy tending the horses.

"She stumbled out back a while ago." The boy lugged two buckets of water down the aisle.

Zeke's heart thudded in his chest. Jacks and Jezebels. He should have paid more attention to her. She drank the beer at the Umatilla like a thirsty cowhand. And he knew she'd never tasted the drink before today.

He stepped into the open alley behind the livery and scanned the area. Nothing moved. Where could she have wandered? A moan filtered through the night air.

Zeke cocked his head.

There it was again. He moved in the direction it appeared to originate. That's when he spotted the privy.

Standing in front of the building, he ran over the proprieties of opening the door. When another moan echoed inside the shack, he grabbed the door and yanked it open. Maeve sat on the wooden bench, her head propped against the wall. Her eyes were closed and she gulped air like an animal taking its last gasp.

"Maeve?" He reached out and shook her arm. "Maeve."

Her eyelids slowly rose.

"Zeke. Did you find my father?" A silly grin brightened her face.

"No. We're getting ready to ride out and find Barton." He grasped her arms, pulling her to a standing position. She flopped against him, wrapping her arms around his neck.

In her condition, he couldn't put her on a horse by herself. He scooped her up in his arms and carried her back into the stable.

"She need a doc?" the stable boy asked, scurrying over as Zeke placed Maeve on his horse.

"No." He swung up behind the drunk woman. "Hand me the reins to that horse." When the boy complied, he nodded his thanks and urged his horse out of the building. They wouldn't be able to travel as fast riding double, but at least he wouldn't have to keep stopping to make sure she was still mounted.

The arm circling the rag doll woman in the saddle in front of him, rested just under her breasts. What would she do if he slid it around and—He groaned. Now wasn't the time. He'd never take advantage or any woman in this state and especially this woman. He wanted her trust. Taking her when she was drunk wasn't showing her any kind of trust.

"Zeke?" Her head smacked back against his chest. Lucky for him she was short enough her head didn't hit him in the chin.

"What?"

"Do you think my father is alive?"

"It's hard to say. Don't think about it, just go to sleep, you'll feel better after you rest." He kissed the top of her head and snuggled her against him.

She sighed and wrapped her arms around his arm like she hugged a puppy or a pillow. Now why couldn't she be this clingy when she was awake?

He shook his head. No, he didn't want a clingy, needy woman. Maeve's independence had captured his attention. Her insistence she needed no one pushed him to prove her otherwise. If she wanted to find out the truth about her father, she needed him. Would she find a reason to slip out of his life once she had the answers? The thought squeezed his chest. He'd find the truth, and then he'd prove to her he was nothing like the man.

To find Loman they needed Barton—who was missing and presumably with Marsh. He ran a hand over his face. Hopefully the information the old man gave him and the specific directions to the whereabouts of Marsh and his group were right. He didn't know why they had Barton. But there wasn't any other explanation for the man's disappearance. He couldn't think of anyone else who would have had a reason to keep Barton from them.

Except Brendan Loman.

Chapter 12

Maeve's stomach was about to erupt. Where was she? And why was she rocking back and forth? She opened her eyes only to clench them shut again when her head pounded harder.

"Stop," she moaned. The rocking stopped, but her head still throbbed.

"She wakes," the deep voice rumbled against her back.

She snapped her head around and started a spasm of pain ricocheting within its confines. The pain encouraged her stomach to heave.

Her feet hit solid ground as a hand roughly flopped her over what felt like a solid rail. She retched upon the ground between two sets of boots. Hers and Zeke's.

His hand lightly brushed loose strands of hair away from her face. "Done?"

She nodded shakily and was rewarded with gentle hands helping her stand. Those hands also drew her backwards.

"Sit."

The word was followed by her body being lowered to a boulder. The whooshing in her ears calmed and the sound of running water registered. Following the sound, she watched Zeke dip a black neckerchief into a stream.

He returned, handing her the wet rag. Maeve wiped her clammy face and then her mouth. He handed her a tin cup of water. She took the offer, swishing water around in her mouth and spitting before taking a long drink. Emptying the cup, she wiped her sleeve across her mouth.

"Thank you," she murmured, looking away from his concerned gaze. How could he show concern when she'd just proven herself weak? She'd known better than to drink two glasses of beer.

Disgusted with herself, she stood. The world spun, and her knees buckled.

"Whoa!" Zeke caught her before she landed in a heap on the ground. She shoved at his hands. She hated weakness.

Tears burned in her eyes and slid down her cheeks. She clenched her fists and ground her teeth. Both acts did nothing to quell the pounding in her head.

"You need to stay put." He crouched in front of her. When she wouldn't look at him, he tilted her chin up. "Hey, what's with the tears?"

He flicked the offending beads of humiliation off her cheeks with his fingers.

"Don't be nice to me."

His head snapped back like she'd slapped him. "Why shouldn't I be nice to you? Because you didn't realize how the beer would affect you?" He slid her over, taking a seat on the boulder next to her. "I've seen men drink less than you did and get sicker." He placed a hand on her chin, making her look at him.

"I hate weak people."

"Honey, you're anything but weak." Zeke grinned and pushed stray hairs behind her ear. His soft touch sent shivers down her neck and tightened her breasts.

She moved her head away from his hand and wished she hadn't. The pounding grew. "I'm weak because I didn't swap my drink with the empty glass of the man beside me like you did."

"You saw that?" Zeke straightened and a frown creased his brow. "Do you think the old man I was questioning did?"

"He was enjoying the whiskey too much to notice. Where are we?" she asked, feeling her stomach start to convulse again.

"Following Eightmile Creek." He followed her when she hurried away from the boulder. His strong hands held her as she emptied her stomach once more.

Zeke helped her back to the boulder and returned to the stream to wash out his neckerchief. He handed it to her along with the tin cup full of water.

"The old man said Marsh liked to hang out at Boyd. I figure if he's got Barton, someone is bound to know."

She swallowed the last of the water. "How do you know so much about following a person?" Ever since Barton didn't show, Zeke had become obsessed with finding the man. And he'd shown he knew how to go about doing it.

"I've helped track down outlaws and murderers." He turned away from her as if the information made him uneasy.

"Is that where you learned to kill a man?" Her soft question jolted Zeke. He didn't want her to know about that side of him. He only wanted to show her gentleness and caring.

When he didn't answer, she took his hand and squeezed.

"I know you would never kill someone without proper cause."

Her conviction in him, made his toes curl. If she knew the rage that pushed him to do the unthinkable, she wouldn't be so quick to side with him.

"That still doesn't make it right." He stood. "Are you able to ride your own horse now?"

Maeve handed him the tin cup and stood on wobbly legs. "I'm ready."

Her confession about weakness was something he already knew about her. Watching her walk to her horse, his admiration for the woman went up another notch. She had more grit than half the men he'd come across in his lifetime.

He hurried up behind her, lifting her onto the saddle. "We'll go slow, but we do need to keep moving."

Her glassy eyes proved her head still gave her fits.

"I'll be fine."

Zeke filled her canteen and hung it from her saddle horn. Cool, fresh water was the only thing he had to help ease her discomfort.

He mounted his horse and continued along the stream. If they continued through the night, they would make Boyd mid morning. His plan was to scout the outlying areas and talk with anyone they came upon. The three knew who they were, and he wasn't about to waltz into town and let them know they were followed. He didn't have the back up of two burly men, only one feisty woman who could handle a gun. He hoped it was enough.

The sun started to skim the tops of the eastern hills when Zeke glanced back at Maeve. She slumped in the saddle, barely holding on. He circled his horse back to her and stopped. It wouldn't hurt to rest the horses and let Maeve take a nap on the ground.

He slipped from his horse and drew her down into his arms. She roused enough to wrap her hands behind his neck. He spied a grassy ravine. The perfect spot for a nap. He carried Maeve and led the two horses. Dropping the reins, the horses went straight to munching on the ankle-high bunchgrass.

Zeke untied the bedroll from Maeve's horse and spread it the best he could with one hand and a woman in his arms. Once it was on the ground, he knelt, placing her on the blanket cushioned with tender, spring grass.

He tied the horses to a couple of trees, providing enough slack for them to eat. Zeke returned to the blanket and the sleeping woman. He sat down, leaned his back against a tree, and pulled his hat over his face.

A nicker and the click of a hammer being pulled back on a pistol, snapped Zeke awake. Fear for Maeve rolled his body toward where she slept. The flat, rough blanket smacked his body. He shot to his feet, taking in the scene of an angry, frightened Maeve being passed between several men.

"Let go of her!" he shouted, disregarding the gun pointed at him and diving into the melee. He grasped Maeve, pushing her behind him as he backed away from the group. "Keep your hands off my wife," he said in a low, commanding voice and stared at each man, defying them to take a step toward him. There was only one who compared to him in size. The rest were average men. But they all had guns pointed at him except for the man with long, blond hair and a sneer.

"We didn't know she was your property," said the unarmed man, pushing his way through the five men smirking like they were ready to take him.

Maeve took offense to being called property. It was bad enough Zeke kept calling her his wife. The men had pulled her from the blanket and a deep sleep, but she now had all her faculties working. She slipped her pistol from the holster and aimed it at the man who'd called her property.

"I'm no man's property." She stepped from behind Zeke and heard his exasperated sigh as she pointed the gun at the man in the front of the pack.

"That so." The man grinned and stepped closer.

Zeke put out his arm to keep her from moving ahead of him. She shot him a sideways glance. The twitch in his jaw proved he was just a tad bit upset with her. She smiled. He had to learn she didn't belong to anyone. Not even him. Her mother taught her a long time ago, she couldn't rely on anyone.

"We're just on our way to Boyd and don't plan on causing you boys any trouble," Zeke said, again pushing her behind him.

She shook her head, planted her feet, and kept the pistol aimed at the man, now standing half way between them and the others.

"I don't plan no trouble." The man spread his hands and aimed a disarming smile their way. "Fellas, put your guns away." The men with the guns aimed at Zeke scowled, but they dropped the muzzles of their rifles to the ground.

She studied the man edging closer. He was a good ten years older than Zeke and not nearly as handsome, but still not hard to look at.

"If you aren't looking for trouble, why did your friends handle my wife?" Zeke's accusing tone did little to wipe the smile from the man's face.

"They were just having a little fun."

"Did that feel like fun to you?" Zeke turned and asked her.

She narrowed her eyes and glared at the intruder. "No, I wouldn't call that fun." She scanned the group gathered behind the man. They were all grinning like they were about to get a gift. She wasn't it.

"I'm tired of every man who gets within arm's reach, grabbing me. The next one is getting a bullet in them." To make them see her point, she squeezed the trigger, shooting at the ground between the closest man's feet. Everyone jumped but Zeke and the man. He just grinned broader.

"Looks like we got us a hellcat boys." He offered his hand. "Ezra Cutter."

She nudged Zeke to extend his hand. It was a good idea to be friends rather than foes when you were outnumbered.

"Zeke Halsey and this is my wife, Maeve," he said, taking the offered hand.

She cringed, but knew it was in her best interest to play out the lie.

"Zeke, Mrs. Halsey." Ezra dropped Zeke's hand and tipped his hat to her. The man seemed cordial enough, but there was something…

"That's a fancy six-shooter you got there, Mrs. Halsey." The way the man said missus sounded almost condescending.

She slid the gun into her holster, and Zeke stepped in front of her, blocking the man's approach.

"We'll be leaving now." Zeke grasped her arm, moving them to the horses without taking his eyes off the group. "Untie the horses," he told her when she bumped into her mare.

Her fingers shook as she tugged on the reins, releasing the knots Zeke had made. Holding her back straight and keeping her hand near her pistol, she handed the gelding's reins to Zeke and swung up onto her saddle. When she was seated, Zeke swung onto his horse.

"I look forward to meeting you again," Ezra's voice carried to them as they urged their horses into a trot.

Her stomach churned. What if those men had

been bent on more than just having fun? They could have killed Zeke without him even knowing they were there and done—she shivered. Why had Zeke stopped?

"Why were we sleeping in that ravine?" she asked, when he finally slowed his horse and twisted in his saddle to scan the trail behind them.

"You fell asleep on your horse." Why did he always have to look so concerned? "I figured a couple hours sleep wouldn't hurt either of us." He fiddled with the reins in his hands. "I'm having trouble keeping you from harm."

"There was no way you could have known those men were around. And you did fine getting us out of there." She pulled on his reins stopping his horse beside hers. "I don't expect you to protect me. I know I'm the only one I can depend on."

His eyes blazed. "You don't have to be. I should have been more vigilant."

She put a hand on his arm. "I appreciate your caring, really I do. But I've had years of being on my own even when I lived with my mother. She taught me I am always on my own."

His large, gloved hand cupped her head. "You'll never be alone as long as I'm around." He tilted his head to keep their hats from knocking together and kissed her.

She wanted to press against him, allow him the solace he sought, but she knew Cutter wasn't far behind. The look on the man's face when he mentioned her gun, hinted at knowledge. Her father gave her the gun. Could this man also have known her father?

Chapter 13

Maeve didn't respond to his kiss. Zeke drew back. She averted her gaze when he searched her eyes.

"Those men still bothering you?" He grasped her shoulders. "I'll do my best to protect you. I promise."

"You can promise all you want, but if those men had wanted to, they could have killed you and," she swallowed, "and done whatever they wanted to me." She licked her lips and wiped at the tears stinging her eyes. "I don't want you getting killed trying to protect me."

"If anything happened to you at the hands of the likes of them, I'd rather be dead then know I didn't try to prevent it." The conviction in his voice squeezed her heart.

"Don't say that."

"Maeve, when will you realize I'm not like your father? When I make a promise, I keep it."

She stiffened her backbone and glared at him.

"How do you know my father hadn't planned to come back to us? From his note, it sounds to me like he was killed or else he would have returned." She had to hold onto that belief. It was the only thing that kept her quiet when Zeke insisted she not say who she was. If her father was murdered, she wanted to find the man and seek revenge. It would also validate the recurring memories of a man who loved her and would not have left her at the mercy of her jealous mother.

"He very well could have planned to come back but met with disaster." Zeke took her gloved hand in his. "I hope for your sake that's what we find. But you have to wonder at why he shot a young man who apparently was at fault for nothing."

"If he shot Marsh's brother. We could be chasing our tails." She couldn't lose faith in her father, not now that she finally believed in him again.

"We aren't going to find out sitting here." He nudged his horse with his heels, and they took off at a trot. With a click of her tongue, the horse under her headed after them. She itched to find Barton and learn more about her father. The man appeared to know a lot. It angered her he disappeared before telling them all he knew.

Zeke leaned on the saddle horn watching the small settlement of Boyd from a grove of alder trees on the north side of the town.

"Are we going to sit here all day?" Maeve's fidgets had her horse dancing.

Her stomach had growled several times in the

hour they sat watching. "I know you're hungry. I just want to make sure Marsh and his buddies aren't in town. Then we can go in, get something to eat, and maybe find a bed."

"I don't see their horses anywhere," she grumbled. He smiled. Losing her dinner from drinking too much and little sleep had made his companion cantankerous.

"Let's head in. If they're here, we'll confront them. Nothing else we can do." He urged his horse out of the trees and headed for Main Street.

The town was small, more of an outpost for the farmers and ranchers to get supplies and provide a church and school for their families. He spotted a large house with a sign "Boarders Welcome".

"Let's try there for food and a bed. I don't see much else." He pointed to the two story home at the end of the street. Maeve nodded and urged her horse forward.

They tied their horses to the rail in front of the yard and followed the dirt path winding through two rows of seedlings popping out of a well-tended bed.

He took hold of Maeve's elbow and knocked on the door. "Remember, we're still married," he whispered when she tried to pull her arm from his grasp.

A woman about Ethan's age opened the door. "Yes?"

He removed his hat. "Ma'am, my wife and I were wondering if you would have a room for us and be willing to fix us a meal."

The woman looked from him to Maeve. Her

mouth formed a disapproving line when her gaze landed on Maeve's holster and gun.

"I don't take in people running from the law." She backed up to shut the door.

He stuck his foot through the opening before she could slam it shut. Her eyes widened in fear. He tugged Maeve forward and entered the house. "Ma'am, we aren't running from the law. My brother is Marshal of Galena. We're actually looking for a friend of ours."

The woman remained skeptical.

Maeve took hold of the woman's hand. "Please, my stomach is aching it's so hungry. We've been traveling all night, and I really need some food and water." Her pleading eyes must have done the trick.

"Come on. I've some bread cooling and coffee's always on."

Zeke breathed a sigh of relief as he followed the two women down a short hall to the back of the house. The kitchen held the heat and aromas from the day's baking. His stomach rumbled and mouth watered.

He held a chair out for Maeve and extended his hand to the woman. "I'm Zeke Halsey and this is Maeve." He refrained from saying my wife, knowing how that rankled his companion. He hoped one day the word would bring her joy.

"Mrs. Langley. Violet Langley." She took his offered hand and reached out to Maeve.

"It's a pleasure to meet you Mrs. Langley," Maeve said, pulling her gloves off and taking the woman's hand.

Mrs. Langley pushed a loaf of bread and a

knife across the table to Maeve. "You cut some slices, and I'll get the coffee."

Zeke took a seat next to Maeve and watched as she sliced the bread and took a bite. Her eyes closed, and he wished he could lean over and lick the crumbs from her lips.

"Who are you looking for?" The woman's words jerked him from his daydreams.

He saw the hesitation in Maeve's eyes. "Jack Marsh."

The woman narrowed her eyes as she set two cups of steaming coffee on the table. "Why would you be looking for that man?"

"We've got some unfinished business with him." Soon as the words came out he realized his mistake.

"Mr. Halsey, anyone with unfinished business with that man, isn't welcome here." Mrs. Langley swung her arm and pointed to the door.

Maeve stood. "Violet, it isn't what you think." She pulled out a chair and motioned for the woman to sit. They stared into one another's eyes a moment before the older woman nodded her head once and sat. He wondered what the exchange had meant.

Taking her seat, Maeve crossed her arms on the table in front of her and leaned forward. "Violet, we believe Jack Marsh has a friend of ours. They both went missing at the same time. This friend has information about my pa, someone I thought walked out on my mother and I years ago." The emotion in her voice had captured the other woman's attention. The vulnerability she displayed surprised him. Maeve had never shown him anything other than a tough, no-nonsense woman. He'd have to think on how she could so easily lay herself out there to this stranger, yet dig a canyon between them.

"The man Marsh has taken may have information about my father's disappearance."

Mrs. Langley placed a hand on Maeve's. "Who is your father?"

Maeve stole a look at him, he shrugged. Might as well see what happens.

"Brendan Loman."

Mrs. Langley pulled back. "I see."

"Did he kill Jack's brother?" Zeke joined the conversation. The woman's trite retort had straightened Maeve's back, and he saw the flint in her eyes sparking.

"Yes. Brendan Loman killed Samuel Marsh. My way of thinking no man should kill, even if the other person doesn't have any scruples."

He raised an eyebrow. This wasn't the way the old man at the saloon painted Samuel Marsh.

"Samuel wasn't the pillar of the community?" He grasped Maeve's trembling hand. She didn't want to believe her father had killed a man. With this new information, it could have been self defense.

"Both them Marsh brothers come from a well-to-do family and could have had a good life. But they both wanted more. Samuel gambled. Neither one was above doing anything to get it." Mrs. Langley pulled the bread loaf to her and sliced, setting another piece in front of each of them.

He didn't like the sound of it. What did Barton know or have that Jack Marsh wanted? And what would he do to get it?

"Does Marsh have a place around here?" Zeke took a bite of the bread.

"The old ranch site. It burned down a year or so after Samuel died. Took both Mr. and Mrs. Marsh." The woman crossed herself. "Just as well, they'd both have died seeing what their remaining son did with his life."

They were getting close, he could feel it. "This ranch, where is it?"

Maeve started to rise. He placed a hand on her shoulder, holding her in the chair. They weren't racing out to the ranch this moment. They both needed sleep.

"East of town about three miles." Mrs. Langley rose. "I'll show you to your room. Dinner will be ready at six."

The woman motioned for them to follow. She moved back down the hall and to the staircase.

"We should go now," Maeve whispered loudly. Zeke held her hand, making her climb the stairs to the second floor.

"No. We haven't had a decent night's sleep in a week. We're going to sleep in a bed and be rested when we find Marsh." He grasped her elbow as Mrs. Langley stopped beside a door.

"This room will be the darkest this time of day." She turned the knob, revealing a pleasant room nearly filled wall to wall with a poster bed.

He propelled Maeve into the room. "Thank you."

"There's fresh water in the pitcher. I'll bring more in a bucket and leave it at the end of the hall." Mrs. Langley pulled the door closed.

When the woman's footsteps faded, he relinquished his hold on Maeve.

"Why couldn't you ask for separate rooms?" Maeve stalked to the stand holding the pitcher and bowl. She unbuckled her holster hanging it from the peg on the wall and tossed her gloves on the bureau.

"That would give the woman even more to wonder about us after we said we were married."

"You didn't really say we were married." Maeve flung her hat at him and poured water into the bowl.

"I wish you would realize I'm not saying or implying it to torture you. I'm trying to keep you safe." He dropped both their hats on the one chair in the room and sat on the edge of the seat to pry his boots off. He glanced at the inviting bed. Sleeping on the floor wasn't going to happen. If they were getting close to Marsh and Barton—and his gut told him they were—he needed to be rested.

Maeve finished washing her face, neck, hands, and arms as far as she could without taking off her blouse. It wasn't so much being thought of as Zeke's wife—it was the closeness it brought. Just like now. One bed—two of them. The weariness had started to creep around Zeke's eyes during the night. He had to rest to keep them on Barton's trail. She tapped the floor with the toe of her boot and grimaced. It was hard. Not even a rug for cushion.

"Take off your boots and clothes." She glanced toward his voice and heat curled in her mid-section. Zeke stood barefoot in his body-hugging red drawers. His muscles stretched the fabric, displaying his body in a way the over clothes could never reveal. The top buttons were undone to mid-chest, displaying a delicious patch of brown, curly hair.

She couldn't speak. When he moved toward her, she couldn't back up. Her feet were rooted, her eyes locked on his.

Zeke took her hand, leading her over to the chair. "Sit."

She sat and he unlaced her boots, drawing them off her feet.

"Do you want me to help you with your clothes?" The huskiness in his voice fluttered her insides. Did she want him to help her undress? And if he did…what then?

The past year, she'd denied the attraction she felt for this man. Glancing into his eyes, she couldn't deny the desire blazing in their brown depths.

Her trembling hands unbuttoned her blouse as he knelt in front of the chair. He growled as she one by one opened the blouse and revealed her silky, lace-edged chemise underneath. His gaze followed the path of her hands. When she reached the waistband of her skirt, he stood, pulling her up in front of him.

He clumsily unfastened the buttons on her skirt and shoved it down over her hips, revealing the lacy, body-hugging drawers he'd purchased for her. She stepped out of the skirt as he pushed the blouse off her shoulders and onto the floor.

"I promise, we won't do anything you don't agree with," he said, before covering her mouth with a hungry kiss.

She leaned into his strong arms. His lips were

full, warm, and wet. His tongue elicited sparks of heat as he skimmed her lips. She sighed, giving him access. Heat scorched to her toes.

Zeke scooped her up. She wrapped her arms around his neck, burying her head against the curve of his jaw. His strength and the gentleness in which he carried her to the bed made her feel treasured. Something she briefly remembered as a child. Before her father disappeared.

He placed her on the bed and lay down beside her. "Maeve, honey, we're both tired. I don't want you giving in to me because you aren't thinking clearly." He turned her to her side, cupped his body behind her, and pulled her tight against him with his other arm. "Sweet dreams," he murmured into her hair.

Her body buzzed with anticipation. His hardness pressed against her backside. His heart raced against her back. Why was he being a gentleman now? How could he get her all stirred up and just go to sleep? She'd never get to sleep with the way her body throbbed.

Spinning under his arm, she faced him. His eyes slowly opened. Placing a hand on either side of his face, she lowered her lips to his. She'd never had a need to learn the art of seduction, but from his intake of breath and flashing eyes, she did something right.

As soon as her lips touched Zeke's, his arms banded around her, pressing her aching breasts against his hard chest. His hands splayed across her bottom, pressing her against his hardness. The pulse between her legs caused her to moan with desire.

He pulled back from the kiss. His dark eyes scanned her face. "You know what we're about to do makes you mine?"

"I won't belong to anyone, but I want this." And she meant it. Making love with Zeke would bring them closer and ease the ache in her, but she would belong to no one. She couldn't let herself care that much, or she would be devastated when he left. And he would.

She tossed her thoughts aside and tangled her hands in his hair, pulling his mouth to hers. She'd take what she wanted. Then he wouldn't feel obligated. She feasted on his lips as his hands massaged her body.

"Damn!" He twisted her onto her back, his body covered hers. All his long, lean muscles rubbed against her. He grasped the bottom of her chemise, pulling it over her head. His gaze fixed on her bare breasts and he stilled. Was something wrong with them? She crossed her arms over her chest. He grasped her wrists, holding her arms above her head.

"Don't you dare cover up, you're beautiful." And he descended. The warm sensation of his mouth covering her sent shudders of delight down her extremities. The rhythm of his tongue flicking the nipple heightened the throbbing between her legs, and then... Oh heavens! He nipped and tugged at the tips with his teeth. Her body bucked pressing her hips against him.

Warm hands slid down her arms, along her sides, and massaged the ache at the juncture of her legs. His hand slipped under her drawers and something slid inside her. Stars danced in her head, and her body hummed.

Nothing had prepared her for the sensations this encounter evoked.

Zeke growled and ran his hands down her hips under her drawers, pushing the garment down her legs and over her feet. She didn't want to be the only one without a stitch of clothing. With shaking, anxious hands, she unbuttoned his red flannels, pushing them off his shoulders, down to his waist. She bit her lip, knelt beside him, and slid her hands down his hips as he'd done to remove her drawers. The sight of his maleness made her throb. She shoved the flannels off his feet and to the floor.

Before she could lie back down, Zeke had her under him. Using his forearms to hold his weight off her, he gazed into her eyes.

"This will be a little uncomfortable at first. But just hang on, and I promise, it'll be worth it." His husky voice and promise conjured up delightful thoughts.

He slid a leg between hers, gently parting them. She had a general idea of what was about to happen. When he pushed against her, she stiffened.

"Shh. It's about there." Zeke kissed her and held his body up off her with one arm while pushing between her legs. She felt him enter and jerked back.

"No, honey, don't think about it. Feel it." He captured a breast in his mouth, and her body trembled as waves of heat rippled. With a quick thrust, he penetrated her maiden barrier and held still.

Maeve shuddered a brief, delicious moment. She wanted more. Wanted him deeper and faster. Clutching his backside, she pulled him close. He began to move slow, gradually picking up the pace. She bit her lip when a hot wave of light shattered her quivering body. Her limp arms slid to the bed and Zeke released.

He collapsed on top of her. The thump of his racing heart and the heat of his body made her smile. He rolled to her side, tucked her up against him, and fell asleep.

She smiled. This was a moment she would savor. When this was over, she would not regret giving herself to Zeke.

Chapter 14

The feel of something warm and smooth invaded his dreams. Zeke moved his hand across a silky expanse of skin. His fingers bumped into a soft mound. He cupped the breast, memorizing the weight and size. Yes, Maeve had given her body to him. But that was all. He would never get enough of her, but he wanted all of her, not just her body. When would she trust him and give him her love? When would she believe he would never leave her?

He wanted to find Barton so Maeve would learn the truth about her father. Find out if he didn't return because he couldn't or wouldn't. He hoped it wasn't the later. He'd never get her to believe he loved her and would never cut out on his responsibilities.

Her low moan as she pushed her breast into his hand hardened him. He never thought the woman who remained so distant would be fulfilling and lusty in bed. Her round bottom snuggled against his hardness. Heat and need shot through him like a flash of lightning.

"You sure you want a go at it again?" he questioned unable to keep the desire out of his voice.

She raised her leg up, bending it back over his hip. He ran his hardness back and forth across her moist center and nearly came when she shuddered and moaned. He thrust into her body and clutched her breasts as he moved inside of her. She gasped and took his full length, rocking back and forth with him.

"Mercy!" she hissed when her body convulsed around him. He thrust deep and hard before spilling. Clinging to her shuddering body, he kissed her neck and continued to play with her hard nipples.

"Marry me. We can do this every day." He let her go when she rolled away.

"Just because I spent the day in your arms doesn't mean I've changed my mind about marrying you or anyone."

There it was. That cold, uncaring tone. How could she be a hellcat in bed one minute and cold as an ice flow the next?

A knock on the door stopped their conversation.

"Dinner will be ready in fifteen minutes," Mrs. Langley called and moved down the hall. At the woman's voice, Maeve bolted from under the covers.

He watched her as she stood next to the bed. She wouldn't meet his eyes. He scanned her naked body. The rosy nipples puckered, her flat stomach fluttered as she breathed. The flare of her hips and long, white legs brought back the thrill of moments before.

He rolled and sat on the opposite edge of the bed, his back to her. "Get dressed. We'll eat and head out after Marsh." He stood and scooped up his clothes from the floor where he'd dropped them.

A breeze whispered past him as she moved to the wash stand. He dressed listening to the splash of water as she cleaned up.

"I'll meet you down in the kitchen." He turned and found her bent over gathering her clothes. The round bottom that had enticed him earlier graced his sight. He swat it playfully. She came up sputtering, and he pulled her naked length against him, planting a long, slow kiss on her enchanting mouth. Her body relaxed, and he set her away from him, exiting the room.

Maeve stood in the middle of the room staring at the closed door. Lightheadedness made her sway on wobbly legs. She collapsed on the chair and wondered at how vulnerable her body became with his touch.

As they made love, she could have sworn her body floated on clouds. The sensations had taken over, and she'd hugged them to her. To experience that elation the rest of her life almost made her say yes, but she knew better. No one stayed in her life. If she leaned on him, Zeke would be gone.

She was better off depending on only herself. Slipping into the lacy undergarments, she smiled. It had only been right Zeke peeled her out of the fancy clothes he bought for her. She scowled. Was that his plan? Show her how he could please her body and then sway her to marry him?

No. He wasn't sneaky. He was the most straight forward man she'd ever met. And if she'd said no, he would have stopped. Her face heated. She'd been wanton. She nearly laughed out loud at the shock, and then admiration on Zeke's face when she initiated their tryst.

Dressed, she buckled her holster and stepped out the door. The smell of roasted meat sent her stomach rumbling. Descending the stairs she heard voices. Did Mrs. Langley have other boarders?

Her boot heels clunked on the wood floor as she made her way to the kitchen. Zeke sat at the table with another man as Mrs. Langley hovered between the stove and table putting dishes before them.

"Here's my wife."

Zeke's emphasis on wife made Maeve blush. What had taken place upstairs could be grounds for a marriage and in some areas made them married.

He stood, extending a hand to draw her near him. "Maeve, this is Jonathan Smalley. He's a friend of Barton."

She stepped up to the stranger, bypassing Zeke. She still tingled in places and didn't want to touch him for fear of craving him.

"Mr. Smalley. How is it you know Mr. Barton?" She took the chair Zeke held for her, but leaned forward, avoiding his hands.

The man flicked a glance at Mrs. Langley. "We worked together a few years back."

She couldn't shake the feeling this man wasn't telling everything. "How come you're here? Barton lives in The Dalles."

Zeke winked at her. Obviously, he liked her questions.

Mr. Smalley cleared his throat, and again, eyed Mrs. Langley. "I'm on an errand for Barton." The man swallowed and avoided her gaze. Either he lied or he wasn't comfortable talking with Mrs. Langley present.

"Would you like to ride out to the Marsh place with us?" Zeke bristled beside her. This man wasn't going to give them any answers until they were alone. And she wanted answers whether Zeke liked it or not.

Mr. Smalley glanced at Zeke. When he didn't show any objection the man smiled. "I wouldn't mind keeping you two company."

Mrs. Langley placed the food on the table. Even though her stomach growled, Maeve took small bites and watched the man shovel food in like he hadn't eaten in days. She glanced at Zeke. He ,too, had one eye on the man, but still managed to clean his plate long before she finished.

"I'll get the horses." Zeke gave her shoulder a squeeze. "Smalley, you better come show me which horse is yours." The tone of his voice gave the man no choice.

She dug into her food with more gusto, knowing Zeke would keep an eye on their lead to Barton.

Zeke scanned the country in front of them. It was too open. He didn't like the fact there wasn't any cover. The only good thing, by the time they arrived at the homestead the sun would have set. Maeve had been right. Once they'd traveled several miles from town, Mr. Smalley opened up some about Barton.

"We met when Barton first come to Oregon." Smalley's face relaxed, and his eyes glazed over as he ventured into his memories.

"Did you ever run across Brendan Loman?" Maeve asked before Zeke could cut her off. They rode with the man and horse between them.

Smalley's head jerked around, and he studied Maeve. The man knew the name. There was no denying this man knew her father. It was written on the etched lines of discontent on the man's forehead.

"How is Brendan?" Smalley asked, in a voice dripping with contempt.

Zeke watched the emotions play across Maeve's face. When it came to her father she could hide nothing. The eagerness in her voice when she asked the question had softened her features. At the man's question, the anger flared in her eyes and her mouth compressed into a straight, hard line.

"I wouldn't know. I've not seen him for ten years," she snapped.

"Have you seen Loman in the last ten years, Smalley?" Zeke watched the man closely for signs he was either lying or knew a whole lot more than he let on. If he had seen the man, they would know Maeve's father was hiding, if not—it left a whole lot of unanswered questions.

The man didn't meet his gaze. "No, I've not seen Brendan Loman in the last ten years."

"How did you come to know him?" Maeve's voice shook as she asked the question. She hung on the man's reply.

"First through Samuel and Jack, then through Barton." The words ground through the man's teeth.

Maeve gasped and Zeke maneuvered his horse between the two.

"How do you know the Marsh brothers?" he asked, keeping between Maeve's horse and Smalley's horse.

"There were several of us rode together." Smalley's eyes narrowed.

"And Loman?"

"He rode with us for a while. Till he killed Samuel."

Zeke's hackles went up. This man was an enemy. Damn! Why hadn't he noticed before he put Maeve in danger? And thinking on it, they'd been following Smalley's directions—which trapped them in a small gully between two hills. The evening light grew dim as the horses carried them from the narrow passage into a larger gorge.

Keeping an eye on the man glaring at Maeve, Zeke stopped his horse at the bank of a stream. He scanned the area cradling the river. Dogwood trees dotted the bank in each direction and sandy cliffs rose away from the water on both sides.

"Water your horse," he said, dismounting and moving toward Maeve. He grasped her about the waist when her feet touched the ground. "He's up to something," he whispered in her ear and backed away. Maeve needed room to use her gun, and he wanted access to his knife.

She nodded and let her horse slurp the water as he watched the man do the same.

Knowing what he knew now, this man showing up at the boarding house wasn't a coincidence. His scalp prickled. They'd been led into a trap. He felt it as sure as his desire for Maeve. Jack Marsh didn't seem smart enough to know they would follow him.

His horse raised its head. Water drizzled out of its mouth before the gelding nickered, and a horse returned the call. He grabbed Maeve's hand, pulling her and the two horses away from the water as he searched the area for their visitors.

"Damn!" The first horse and rider to come into view set his gut twisting. It was Cutter and his bunch. He hadn't liked the way the man eyed Maeve at their first meeting. Or the way she'd been distracted after that meeting.

"Well, if it isn't Mr. and Mrs. Halsey. Look what we found, boys." Cutter stopped his horse far enough back he could keep them in view.

The men behind him snickered.

"You bypassed Boyd." Cutter turned to his men. "Isn't that where they said they was goin'?"

The men nodded and agreed vocally.

"Now, what are you doing clear out here?" Cutter leaned on his saddle horn and stared at Maeve.

Zeke stepped between the two. The sneaky bastard, Smalley, walked up to Cutter.

"They're headed to see Jack Marsh." The humor in Smalley's voice tightened Zeke's gut. Maeve's exasperated sigh feathered warm breath across his back.

"Well then," Cutter raised his arms and all of his men pointed guns at them, "why didn't you say so. We'd be more than happy to escort you to Jack."

Smalley slapped his hat against his thigh. "And you know what? You was right. She's Loman's daughter!" The elation in the man's voice sent shards of ice through Zeke's limbs.

Before he could register Maeve's intentions, she stepped from behind him, her hands fisted on her hips.

"How did you know I was Brendan Loman's daughter?" Maeve wasn't about to hide behind Zeke when the man with answers to her father sat not twenty feet away.

"By that gun hanging so pretty from your hip." Cutter's gaze drifted from her face down her neck, lingered on her breasts, and over to her left hip where the pistol her pa gave her rested in the holster. His perusal didn't arouse her like Zeke's eyes devouring her. This man's gaze soured her belly.

"That's absurd!" Her pa gave her this gun when she was ten, and she hadn't let it out of her sight since. How could they know it had belonged to her father?

"When I first met your pa he had a matched set. About a year later he started using only one pistol. Said he lost the other one in a poker match." Cutter ran his gaze over her again. "I think he gave it to his pretty, little girl to keep big, bad men away." The mob behind him roared with laughter. A chill that had nothing to do with the weather seeped to her bones.

Zeke once again placed his body between her and the men. His chivalrous act had become annoying. She had to watch the men in order to help. Shielding her from them also shielded her from acting.

She put a hand on his arm and stepped up beside him. "I can't use my gun standing behind you," she said in a low voice.

"Is that why you followed us? You recognized the gun." The control in Zeke's voice didn't surprise her. He'd proven on more than one occasion it took a lot to fluster him.

"That and wanting to see how far from the tree that juicy apple standing next to you fell." Cutter still sat hunched over the saddle horn where his arms rested.

She wondered what her father had done while riding with these men. Her gut said it wasn't honest. She shot a glance at Zeke. His gaze didn't waver in intensity or direction, but his jaw clenched.

"Round 'em up boys," Cutter growled and the mob surged forward, swarming around her and Zeke. Smalley snatched her gun from her grasp when Zeke pulled her against him with one hand and back-handed the first man who came close to them.

"Zeke, no. We can't fight all of them." If they went along, there might be a chance of escape. His hand raised again and several guns clicked.

"No! Don't shoot!" she shrieked and grabbed at Zeke's arm, drawing it back down to his side.

"You got a wise woman there, Halsey." Cutter rode up next to them. "Mount up. Jack's waiting."

Chapter 15

Rope bit into Zeke's wrists as he watched Cutter lead Maeve's horse while the large man, Mac, led his horse. There were three men on horseback in between he and Maeve. Anger at his stupidity for walking into the mess and not hanging onto Maeve ate at him like a crow picking at a carcass.

If Marsh had Barton, they would get their chance to talk to the man. But chances were Barton was one of this band of outlaws. Smalley was part of this group, and he admitted to meeting Barton and Loman through this group. Zeke's eyebrow twitched when trouble was coming and right now it fluttered like a goddamn hummingbird's wing.

Cutter stopped his horse at the top of a rise. All the riders urged their horses forward and peered down. The moon sat high in all its glory, illuminating a small valley below. Nearly fifty head of horses grazed in the moonlight. Three dark spots shaped like shacks lined a stream reflecting the moon's rays in the middle of the valley.

"Jack's place," Cutter said with a smirk. He laid a hand on Maeve's knee.

"Keep your filthy hands off her." Zeke lunged at the man. A gun clicked, and a hard, round barrel jabbed in his ribs. He wouldn't be any good to Maeve dead. He settled back on his horse. His eyebrow twitched like the wings of a wasp. It was going to be hell watching that pole cat put his hands on his woman.

Maeve pushed the hand off her knee. She heard Zeke's growl and worried he'd do something stupid. The click of a pistol cylinder jerked her head around. Zeke had settled back in the saddle, but the fury in his eyes said it was only a matter of time before he lost control.

She had to find a way to stay in Cutter's graces to learn all she could about her father, and yet, keep Zeke from getting killed.

The horses started down the slope. She shoved her feet firmly in the stirrups and leaned back. Since she didn't have to steer the horse, she scrutinized the valley, noting the buildings and the shortest distance to the trees. She and Zeke would get away.

The group surrounding them counted six men. Smalley mentioned hurrying ahead to scout things out. But she noticed he went a different direction than the rest of them followed. She was pretty sure the two that followed Marsh would be with him. How many others might there be? She wished she had her gun. Without it they had a formidable number to fight.

She smiled. They didn't know about Zeke's knife. That would be the only weapon they had when they made a run for it.

A man to her right let out a string of shrill whistles. Three men stepped out of the largest of the shacks. Marsh and his cronies. No other heads popped out anywhere. That meant nine outlaws. Her chest squeezed. Not great odds, but better than she'd feared.

She glanced back at Zeke. His gaze flicked to her. The rest of his face remained immobile as a boulder. She tried to smile, but couldn't find a reason. They were prisoners.

"What'cha bring them here for?" Marsh asked, stepping up to her horse.

Cutter handed her pistol down to Marsh. "I thought you'd like the daughter of the man who killed Samuel."

She sucked in air as Marsh jerked his head and glared at her. He took the gun and turned his attention on the smoothly-worn handle.

"What's your name?" Marsh asked, grabbing her arm and pulling her down from the horse.

"Maeve Halsey and get your hands off her!" growled Zeke, urging his horse forward.

The chorus of clicking hammers spiraled fear into her chest.

"Zeke, he's not hurting me." She glanced over her shoulder at the man defending her. The torture in his eyes called to her heart. Whatever happened, he had to get out of this situation unscathed. She wasn't sure if maintaining the charade of their marriage would save her, but it would help Zeke believe he'd done everything he could.

She squared her shoulders and glared at the man a few inches shorter than herself. "I'm Brendan Loman's daughter." Zeke's frustrated growl set her resolve up a notch.

"We're here seeking information about my father. It seems most of you knew him. I'd like to learn more about him."

All the men had dismounted, including Zeke. She backed up, pressing against his unyielding body. The strength she garnered from him didn't surprise her.

"I'd appreciate your cooperation. I'm here to find out why my father always left for long stretches of time." The men sent furtive glances amongst themselves. She grasped Zeke's hand. "And then we'll leave."

Cutter stepped forward. A smirk twitched the corner of his mouth. "Telling you about your pa might not look too favorable on us."

Zeke squeezed her hand. She glanced up under his hat brim to his smoldering eyes. There had to be a way to learn the truth and get out of this alive.

"What if we promise to leave here and never mention a word about you or whatever you tell us?" The pleading tone in her voice made her cringe.

Cutter and Marsh both threw their heads back and laughed. She had to remember they weren't dealing with law-abiding men. These men could possibly have murdered her father and Barton.

"Put him in that shack," Cutter waved away Zeke and clutched her arm.

Zeke ripped her arm from Cutter's grasp and landed a firm blow to the man's belly. She backed away as the man doubled over. Before she could get her hands on a gun, three men jumped on Zeke while the others drew their weapons. Zeke stopped struggling. He glared at Cutter as the men held him.

Cutter straightened, his face pinched in pain. He glared at Zeke. "You'd be dead if I didn't want this woman to cooperate." The outlaw snaked an arm around her waist, dragging her to the middle, larger shack. He turned, glaring at Zeke and tightening his hold on her. "You behave yourself, and she won't be harmed."

Maeve's stomach clenched as three men struggled to push a raging Zeke through the door of a shack on the far side. Her heart ached when he took a nasty hit. He would be submitted to far worse treatment than she. All because of his devotion to her. She ground her teeth with determination. She'd find a way to get to him and get out of this valley.

Zeke seethed. Jacks and Jezebels. He was trussed up like a hog on a spit, and Maeve was in a shack with a man who had no scruples. He rocked the chair. If he couldn't loosen the ropes, he might be able to break the chair, and then get loose.

He tipped. The chair rested on two legs for what seemed an eternity and crashed to the floor. Oomph. Air whooshed out of him. The brim of his hat saved his head from ramming into the floor. Gulping air, he wiggled hands, feet, then arms and legs. Nothing. The rope still cut into him. His effort got him nowhere, except stuck on his side on the dirt floor.

What was Cutter doing with Maeve? The

torment of all the images in his head made his eyebrow twitch and his head pound. He had to get free. Had to get them out of here.

Scanning the shack, a shiny object caught his attention. A knife rested on a piece of wood by the stove. If he scooted over, he'd be able to grasp the weapon in his hands behind his back. Flexing his body and pushing with a foot against the hard, packed dirt, he maneuvered slowly across the floor. He stopped when the sound of footsteps approached. He was vulnerable on his side all trussed up.

Holding his breath and listening, he waited. The footfalls stopped outside the door then faded away. Huffing and straining, he began to slither across the floor once more. He bumped the wood with his foot and scooted down, feeling with his hands for the knife. The wooden hilt touched the tips of his fingers. Pushing closer, the handle pushed against his back. He clutched the knife and started to saw at the rope about his arms.

Voices murmured outside the door.

Maeve rubbed her hands up and down her arms. Once Cutter closed the door behind him, fear crept up her spine like a cold winter wind. That fear doubled when she thought of the three men practically carrying Zeke away. Would they hurt him? This whole trip was for her. To learn about her father. However, the more she dug, she feared she jeopardized not only her life but Zeke's.

"Sit down. And I'll tell you about Irish." Cutter pulled out a chair at the small table in the middle of the room.

She frowned and took the offered seat. "Who was Irish?"

"Your father. He rode with the gang about four months before he shot Samuel."

No. Her father wasn't an outlaw. The man she remembered held high esteem for the law. He wouldn't steal and kill. "I don't believe you."

Cutter snickered. "Well, you better, cuz, I know. I'd only been with the gang about a year when your father helped us out of a tight spot. We'd robbed a bank and were holed up shootin' it out with the town. Not sure how Irish pulled it off, but he got us out the back and away from that town before the marshal knew we was gone." The respect in the man's voice repulsed her.

"We gave him a cut and offered him to stay with us. Samuel was the oldest until your pa joined. Wasn't long before Irish had a fair amount of the men hanging on his words and ignoring Samuel."

"Pa killed him in self-defense then." She couldn't help but feel a little bit vindicated.

"Naw. Your pa just flat out shot Samuel." Cutter ran a hand over his whiskered face. "Damnedest thing. We was all in town playing poker and rousting the women." Cutter ran his gaze over her chest and licked his lips.

She shuddered and he grinned.

"What happened when you were in town?"

"Samuel disappeared and then so did your pa. Didn't think much about it at the time. I was busy with a pretty wench." He winked and placed a hand on her knee. She shoved the offending hand away.

"I'm married and in case you didn't notice…
my husband is of the jealous sort."

Cutter snorted. "You've got your pa's spit
that's for sure."

"So what happened that night?"

"All of a sudden, Mac came running into the
saloon where I was sampling and said Irish just
gunned down Samuel. Before we could get to them,
the marshal had your pa in custody." Cutter stood
and walked to the pot-bellied stove heating the
room to a sweltering level. He poured two cups of
coffee and returned to the table.

"What happened to my pa?" She wrapped her
hands around the cup. If her father had hanged
wouldn't they have notified her mother? Is that
why she'd refused to tell her daughter the truth?
Could her mother have possibly shown an inkling
of compassion for her child?

"We had it all set up to break him out, only
Jack went all loco and took off with Irish." Cutter
looked her dead in the eyes. "I don't know for sure,
but I'd bet he killed your pa."

"So you never saw the body?" She had to hang
onto the idea her father might still be out there.
Hiding.

Cutter shook his head. "Marsh is tetched and
he an' his brother were close. I may not have seen
a body, and Marsh never boasted, but he came back
by himself all peaceful. Like he'd conquered the
devil that'd been hounding him." He scanned her
and leered. "If not for me, he'd have put a bullet
through you soon as he knew you were a Loman."

A cry erupted from her constricted throat. Her
father was dead. Even though after reading his

letter she believed that had been his fate, hearing it wracked her with sadness. She wanted Zeke. Wanted his strong arms around her.

"I need to see Zeke." Her strangled voice filled with emotions she didn't want a stranger privy to. "Please."

Cutter stood, grabbed her by the arm and pulled her out of the shack toward the one where they'd delivered the man she was learning to lean on.

Voices and footsteps approached. Zeke remained trussed up on the floor and more vulnerable than a child. The knife had proved too dull to cut paper let alone the rope binding him. Whoever it was, they weren't going to kill him without a fight.

The door opened. The moonlight behind the person blinded him for a moment.

"Zeke." The sweet voice chased away his rage. The door closed, and Maeve hurried toward him.

"Let me help you up."

"Just grab my knife and cut the ropes." The gentle touch of her hands skimming down the side of his leg to find the hilt of the knife in his boot warmed his heart and his body.

The ropes gave way and he surged to his feet, pulling her into his arms. "I thought—you don't want to know what I thought." He lowered his lips to her upturned mouth. Maeve sagged against him. Her kiss seemed melancholy rather than rapturous.

He held her head in his hands. "What's wrong?"

"Cutter told me. My father—" Tears formed in her sad, blue eyes and slid down her cheeks. "He rode with this gang and killed Samuel. And," she took a deep breath, "Cutter believes Jack killed Pa." She wrapped her arms around him. "He's dead. And," she hiccupped, "he was an outlaw."

He hugged her trembling body to him. He'd feared once she gained the knowledge of her father, she'd withdraw. But she clung to him, taking the sympathy he had to offer. His heart swelled. Did she finally realize she could need someone and still remain strong? There wasn't time to consider any of this. They had to leave.

"Why did Cutter let you come see me?" He kept one arm around her as he moved to look out the window.

"Because I asked." She wiped at the tears and peered out the window as well.

He stared at her. "You just asked and he let you come see me?" The outlaw didn't make any sense.

She nodded her head. The dawning of how inconceivable the idea showed on her face. "He's up to something."

Nothing moved in front of the shack. But a man sat not ten feet from the door, leaning against a rock, and cradling a rifle in his lap.

"Did he say how long you could stay?" He pulled her to the back of the building and looked for a peephole in the boards.

"No. I just asked to see you, and he led me over here." Maeve pressed her face against a board. "Looks like they plan to go somewhere. There's fresh horses saddled."

He pressed his face against a hole higher on the wall. "I count nine horses. That would be all of them." He didn't want to voice the thoughts in his head. Nine horses meant he and Maeve wouldn't be leaving.

Zeke pulled her to him, clinging to her scent and strength. If they were to make it out alive it would take strategy and quick thinking.

"We need to come up with a plan. Fast." He led her to the bed and sat, drawing her down beside him. "Did you notice where the men were located when you walked here?"

"Some." Maeve scrunched her face. "I was upset and didn't pay proper attention."

Her declaration swelled his heart. He clasped her hands in his. "Once we get out of this mess, will you marry me?" He held his breath. This wasn't the time or place for such a question, but he had to ask.

Maeve wanted to say 'yes'. Wanted to give that hope to Zeke. However, she'd sampled what it was like to make love to him and had no doubt whether they were married or not she could arouse him to the point where he'd make love to her again. She didn't need a man to take care of her. Her mother had depended on a man and look how she'd ended up. Alone and destitute.

She shook her head. His mouth formed a straight line. The look in his eyes said he was nowhere near defeated.

Zeke's large hand cupped the back of her head, and his mouth descended on hers. His lips scorched, and his tongue gently stroked her lips, building passion. She didn't want to fight the emotions. Her hands wound into his hair, pulling him closer. The heat of the kiss seared her skin and made her center throb.

She climbed onto his lap. His hand cupped a breast, and her nipple hardened. A delectable ache formed in her womb as his hands squeezed. He nibbled his way down her neck to the opening of her blouse. The desire building in her mid-section burned hot and fast.

She wanted him. Now.

Her hands fumbled with the button on his pants.

"Hey, not so fast." Zeke captured her hands. "We should find a way out of here."

"We can get away after they leave." She fluttered her eyelashes and licked her lips. The desire in his dark eyes made her nipples tingle.

"Someone could walk in at any minute." Zeke scanned the room. The board that barred the door shut was missing. He kissed Maeve and stood. Using the rope he'd been tied with, he tied the bracket on the door to the bracket on the wall. They'd know when someone tried to come in.

He returned to the bed. The woman he'd go to his grave protecting reclined on the bed with the buttons of her blouse undone and her lacey chemise barely containing her breasts.

"You're gonna be the death of me," he said, lowering his body over the top of hers and nuzzling her offering. His desire for her strained against his Levis.

"Hmmm... but what a way to go." She cocked an eyebrow and stroked his growing appendage through the clothing.

To keep her occupied, he pushed the chemise down and suckled first one and then the other breast. His knee rubbed against the juncture of her legs. Maeve's hips rose up to meet each stroke.

He reached between, fumbling with the buttons on her skirt.

The door creaked.

The sound jolted his body like a bucket of cold water.

<h1 style="text-align:center">Chapter 16</h1>

He rolled off Maeve, shielding her with his body as the door popped off the hinges.

Smirking, Cutter entered the room. "Well, what do we have here? You're lucky you were fornicatin' and not tryin' to run."

Zeke rose off the bed, ready to take the man down.

The barrel of a gun pointed at them before he had time to react. "Back off," Cutter snarled. "Mrs. Halsey, get over here." He cocked the pistol. "Now, or I shoot your man."

Zeke put out a hand to stop her, but Maeve rushed by, fastening the top button on her blouse. Her embarrassment made his heart ache. He should have resisted. He should have stayed vigilant. Damn. His lust put them in danger, again.

Cutter stepped aside, allowing three men to enter the building. "Tie his hands and escort him to the other shack." The man grasped Maeve's arm, making her grimace. Anger and fear for her propelled Zeke out of the men's grasp and straight for Cutter.

The pistol pointed at Maeve stopped him cold.

"You behave or I'll shoot your wife. She means nothing to me."

He'd seen expressionless eyes before. On the faces of killers. The man meant every word. He'd kill Maeve and not even consider he'd done anything wrong.

"Make sure he's tied up tight. If I find out you're causing problems," he cocked the gun still against Maeve's heaving side, "she's dead."

Cutter pulled Maeve out of the way as the men shoved and prodded Zeke out the door. He glanced back to see where the outlaw took Maeve and got cold-cocked.

Maeve struggled to get free when she saw the man hit Zeke for no reason.

"Uh, uh, uh, same goes for you. Do as I say or your man will be shot." Cutter pinched the inside of her arm, pulling her to the saddled horses. "We're going for a ride. We have some money to withdraw. And you're going to help us."

All but one of the men who took Zeke away returned to the horses.

"Mount up," Cutter ordered, motioning for her to get on a horse. After she mounted, he pulled her hands behind her and tied them.

"Don't want you getting any smart ideas. And remember, you don't do as I say—when we get back here—I'll personally put a bullet through your man's head."

Fear clenched her heart. She didn't mind dying, but she'd do everything in her power to keep

Zeke alive.

Maeve tried to relieve the throbbing in her backside by standing in the stirrups. With her hands tied behind her back, her balance was off, and she plopped back down, further inflaming her sore muscles.

They kept a steady trot-and-walk pattern all night. Finally, Cutter stopped the group at a shabby ranch house. Everyone dismounted, unsaddled, and put their saddles on fresh horses before heading out at a trot once more. Cutter led her horse. He seemed to take pleasure in making sure she didn't go thirsty and didn't eat the dust like those riding in the back of the group.

Marsh rode close and sneered at her. Her skin prickled. She swayed away from the hostile man. He glared once more before nudging his horse even with Cutter. The two men slowed the horses and carried on a heated conversation. She leaned forward, hoping to catch a hint of where they were headed.

"What you got to bring her along for?" Marsh asked, looking over his shoulder. Hatred sparked in his eyes.

"She's gonna keep me alive and be my entertainment." The chuckle Cutter emitted sent a chill down her back.

"What' cha gonna do with her while we're gettin' the payroll? Someone will notice a woman tied to a horse."

"She's going to be the first one entering the bank. No one's gonna shoot at a woman."

"I still say we should just shoot her." Marsh's voice raised an octave.

"Like you did her pa?"

Marsh didn't answer. The silence was his condemnation. She knew in that instance he murdered her pa.

She gulped and wondered if she would make it back to Zeke alive, and if she didn't would Cutter spare him?

The sun came up, warming her chilled body. Her eyelids felt weighted. Her body slumped...

Zeke moved his head and moaned. Why'd the bastard hit him? All he did was look back at Maeve. Maeve. Forcing his eyes open, he scrutinized his surroundings through blurry vision. It was a different shack. Someone breathed behind him. Craning his neck, he could make out a man tied to a chair. He blinked and focused. The clothing appeared expensive.

"Barton?" he whispered unsure if an outlaw stood guard on the other side of the door.

"Yeah. Wondered when you were going to come around." Barton's weary voice made him wonder how the man had been treated. "Where's Maeve?"

The question speared his heart. "I don't know. When I tried to see where Cutter took her some bastard knocked me out."

"Horses left here shortly after they brought you in."

"Nine." That meant either Maeve was in another shack trussed up like them or...Rage took hold of him like a dog shaking a varmint. "Has anyone checked on us?"

"Yeah, the same guy every time and it's been hours. I think he's the only one here." Barton coughed. His chair was close enough the man's spasms shook Zeke's chair.

"I'm going to try and get turned." Zeke flexed his calf. His knife was still there. "I've got a knife in my boot." He rocked the chair back and forth, pivoting on the legs. Inch by inch, he turned the chair. Sweat dripped down his temples when he finally had his leg next to the man's hands.

"Feel with your hands. Find the top of my boot."

Barton strained, stretching his fingers, brushing the top of Zeke's boot.

"I'll try to raise my foot." Tipping the chair onto the back legs, he brought his boot closer to Barton. The man finally grasped the hilt, and Zeke set the chair back on four legs.

"I'll turn back around. See if you can cut the ropes on my hands." He started the slow motion of turning the chair.

"I got it." Barton had cut the ropes binding his hands and was already working on the ones around his body. When he was free, he started slicing through the rope tethering Zeke to the chair.

Zeke shot to his feet, grabbed his knife from Barton, and crossed the room. Peering out the window, he spotted their guard. The man looked asleep the way he leaned on the butt of his rifle. Without consulting Barton, he eased out the door and behind the sentry.

He wrapped an arm around the man's throat,

kicked the rifle aside, and shoved the tip of his knife into the man's side.

"Where did Cutter take my wife?" he growled, giving the knife a twist to let his hostage feel the sharp point.

"Don't know." The man spat.

"Like hell you don't." He tightened his hold on the man's neck and pushed more with the knife.

"You...kill... me...you'll...never...find...out." His voice was barely audible as he gasped for air.

"That's true," Barton said, grasping the man's thumbs, forcing Zeke to move, and jerking the outlaw's arms behind him. The man cried out in pain. Zeke grinned and took note of how quickly and easily the smaller man apprehended the larger one.

"But, we don't have to kill you to get the answers we want." Barton continued to hold the man's thumbs as he maneuvered the man back into the shack. With just a small move on Barton's part the man cried out again.

"How'd you do that?" Zeke asked, hoping to learn something new.

"You just bend his thumb," the man cried out again, "like that." Barton demonstrated the hold and stepped to the side. "Care to try? Though do be careful, if it's done wrong you can break the bones."

The outlaw looked at him standing a head taller than Barton and shook his head. "He took her to Monument."

Barton muttered an oath.

"You know why?" He shoved the pathetic outlaw into the chair and turned to Barton.

"Yeah. And why they've had me tied up here."

Barton started pacing. "I should've known Smalley couldn't be trusted."

"I thought you two were friends? That's what he insinuated." Zeke shoved a sock he found under the cot into the outlaw's mouth and tied the man's hands behind his back.

"Not friends. But associates. I've believed for a while now he was working both sides. Now I know for sure." Barton ran a hand through his gray hair.

"Were you and Loman associates?" He still didn't know what to think about the man in front of him and the man Maeve so desperately wanted to learn about.

"Yes. And friends." Barton stopped. "Does Marsh know about Miss Loman?"

Fear stuck in Zeke's throat. He swallowed and nodded his head. "Smalley and Cutter made sure he knew."

Barton paced again. "I don't think they'll do anything to her until they finish what they've set out to do." He looked around the shack. "Let's see what we can find to eat, and I'll fill you in on what I think is happening."

A hard body held her, but it wasn't as large as Zeke. Maeve opened her eyes and stared into a face that sent shivers down her spine.

"Well, Sleeping Beauty, I see you decided to wake up in time to help us." Cutter's sarcastic voice snapped her spine straight. She used her head to shove away from his chest, since her hands were still bound behind her, and backed into a horse.

The animal sidestepped, and she struggled to

remain standing. The men around her laughed. She scanned the group, wincing at her aching shoulders and throbbing wrists. Where was she? And how did she come to be standing when the last thing she remembered was riding a horse?

She'd fallen asleep on the horse. How did she manage to stay on? She shivered at the memory of Cutter holding her so intimately. Surely, she would've woke up if he'd pulled her onto his horse. She glanced at the horse behind her. It was the last one she'd been riding. Confusion muddled her thinking.

Why were they stopped? She pivoted and spotted the reason. A wide river blocked their path. At least Cutter had the decency to wake her before dragging her horse through the river.

She studied her shadow. It was still morning. She squinted and peered across the water. A well-worn path, possibly a road appeared on the other side.

"Where are we?" she asked. Cutter turned from Smalley who'd just joined them.

"We are on the road to riches." He grasped her about the waist, hoisting her onto the horse.

Maeve glared down at him. She wanted to kick him in the teeth, but knew she wouldn't live to do it again, and the man would go back and shoot Zeke. Taking out her frustration wasn't worth Zeke dying.

Even though Barton didn't expect anyone to return during the night, Zeke couldn't sleep. Maeve was on her way to Monument with a killer.

"She'll be fine. She's a smart woman," Barton said from the bed where he'd moments before been snoring.

"She also has a temper. One she has trouble keeping a handle on." He smiled thinking of all the times she'd unleashed it on him.

"Sounds like her father's Irish came through." Barton chuckled.

"You never did tell me exactly how you knew Loman." He'd been waiting all night for the man to divulge what he knew.

"We worked together before he came up missing."

"Maeve said Cutter told her he figured Marsh killed him." Zeke walked to the stove and poured another cup of coffee.

"Yeah, before I had a chance to explain everything to the Sheriff, Marsh busted Brendan out of jail and disappeared." Barton tugged on his mustache. "I tried to find them, but Brendan was the tracker, not me."

"Explain what?" He watched the man. His face appeared older in the gray light of dawn. His eyes held regret.

"That Brendan was working for the Pinkerton's and had killed Samuel Marsh to prevent an assassination of a railroad tycoon who had stopped over in The Dalles at the time."

Zeke spit his coffee across the table. "He was what?"

"A Pinkerton agent assigned to the West. I was his contact for assignments."

"Why didn't he tell his wife what he did?" He pulled his chair closer to the bed and leaned forward, his arms on his knees.

"Brendan infiltrated the Molly Maguires in Pennsylvania. His involvement brought the lot of them down. He had to get out of the East or die. So he loaded up his wife and daughter and came out here. He tried to lead a normal life, but the excitement of bringing in someone breaking the law was something he couldn't leave behind."

"He told his wife he was prospecting for gold. Maeve believes his greed kept him from them and was eventually his death." Zeke stared at the man. She'd thwarted his advances because of a lie. One her father fabricated to keep his family safe.

"Mrs. Loman had a tendency to not be able to keep a confidence. She nearly got Brendan, and I believe your relative, killed during the war."

He stared at the man. "What do you mean my relative?"

"I would imagine he was a cousin, because there is a very strong family resemblance." Barton stood and stretched.

"That would explain it!" Zeke grinned. He knew his father hadn't been in the war. "We showed Mrs. Loman a tintype of my parents because Maeve insisted my father was her uncle from what her father had told her." He couldn't stop grinning he was so relieved. "Mrs. Loman said they weren't related, but insisted that my father had been in the war with Loman." He frowned. "It must have been my uncle's oldest son. After the war, they never heard from him again."

Barton put a hand on his shoulder. "I can't help you there. I came west before that was all settled." He moved to the stove and poured a cup of coffee.

"Why did Loman join with Marsh and Cutter?"

"We were paid to guard Henry Villard, a railroad magnate, when he was in our area. We had people in all the saloons and found out Samuel Marsh was the person paid to kill Villard. Brendan learned all he could about the group and made his way into the gang to keep an eye on Samuel." Barton sat at the table. "The night Brendan shot Samuel, the young man walked straight toward Villard in a gambling establishment with his gun drawn." The remorse in Barton's eyes said it all. "I hurried to the jail as soon as I heard, but Jack had already busted Brendan out."

"Did Jack know Loman was a spy?"

"I honestly don't know." Barton took a sip from his cup.

Zeke stared at the man. He feared not only for Maeve being the daughter of the man who killed Samuel, but if they knew he was a spy—how would they treat her?

Chapter 17

Maeve stood in the middle of the bank lobby. The scene around her resembled any other time she'd entered a bank. Except for the gun barrel jabbed in her back. Cutter had untied her hands. She rubbed at her raw wrists and scanned the room for a way to not get shot, but hinder the robbery.

"Hand over the bridge payroll and no one gets hurt," Cutter shouted, causing the bank tellers to scurry. She felt the gun leave her back at the same moment she recognized Zeke's sister-in-law. The woman stood not five feet from her, protectively clutching her protruding stomach.

Their eyes met, and Darcy sank to the floor. Maeve hurried to her. "They have Zeke outside of Boyd. Marsh Ranch," she whispered before being yanked away.

"Git over here. Don't be cozying up to no one." Cutter shoved the gun in her side again and pulled her to the door. "Grab them bags, boys," he called and motioned with his head for the others to leave the building.

When the last man exited, Cutter gripped her arm and made a show of shoving the gun tighter against her side. She watched the frightened faces of the people in the bank as Cutter's menacing voice boomed, "If anyone follows, I'll shoot this woman and them." Her heart sank at the cowardly way the people backed up. All but Darcy. Her gaze never flinched, nor did she back away. Before Cutter yanked her out the door, Darcy gave her a brief nod.

Instead of letting her mount her own horse, he threw her on his horse and jumped up behind. The whole lot of them raced down the street. She looked back as Gil ran into the bank. If he followed, she hoped he found Zeke before the man clutching her killed him.

They rode at a lope for a couple of miles before stopping. Cutter dismounted and pulled her down off his winded horse.

"Git on your horse," he ordered and turned to the others. "You three head east, you three head north, and we'll meet you back at Jack's in two days."

The men nodded and started off in their given directions. That left her alone with Marsh and Cutter. The glares she received from Marsh made her want to hide behind Cutter, even though he wasn't any better.

Maeve thought about kicking the horse and heading back to town, but knew she'd be shot in the back and the man would head straight for Zeke and kill him before anyone could stop him.

"Since you done such a fine job at the bank, I'll tie your hands in front, though I'm gonna miss lookin' back and seeing these breasts of yours poked out and beggin' to be touched." She flinched as Cutter fondled the breast closest to him. He laughed and pulled her hands together, tying them a bit looser than before.

"I think we should just shoot her," Marsh said, urging his horse up next to hers.

"We aren't free yet. If we're followed, we need her for a shield. Besides," Cutter winked at her, "she's come'n around to likin' me. I can tell."

Bile rose in her throat as the man ran his hand down her leg before he mounted his horse.

Cutter set out at a trot, dragging her horse behind him. Marsh brought up the rear. She could feel his hatred drilling into her back. They kept up the pace after crossing the river. The route was different. Was it longer of shorter than the one they took on the way to the robbery?

She hoped shorter. The thought of spending time with the two men evoked scenarios that all ended with both she and Zeke dead. Cutter wouldn't outright kill her. He'd torture her and use her body before he pulled the trigger. She'd figured him out, but Marsh—he seethed with hatred. Hatred aimed at her. He could blow up at any minute, and Cutter wouldn't be able to stop him. Maeve shuddered. She wished for Zeke's strong arms around her one more time.

Zeke stalked back and forth in the sparse cluster of cottonwood trees where he, Barton, and the outlaw waited for the return of the gang. He didn't want to spend another night worrying about Maeve, if she was alive, if Cutter raped her. The thought pounded in his head. Clenching his fists at his side, he thought of all the things he should have done to keep her safe.

"I doubt they'll return until tomorrow." Barton sat on a rock whittling on a stick.

"How can you sit there so patient, knowing they used you to get their hands on the bridge pay-roll?" Zeke stopped in front of the man.

Barton stopped whittling, turning his gaze on Zeke. "I can't foresee the future. If I could, my inklings about Smalley would have told me he wasn't to be trusted. I can't think about what if's only construct ways to right the wrongs that have been done."

He motioned to the path Zeke's pacing had created. "Besides worrying and stomping about like a wounded bear isn't going to get them here any earlier. Or conserve my energy for when they do arrive." Barton pointed to a stump. "Sit. Or better yet, roll out a blanket and rest. I know you didn't sleep at all last night." Sympathy softened Barton's eyes. "She'll be fine. She loves you and will do whatever Cutter asks to see no harm comes to you."

"She loves me?" He sat down. Did she really? "How the hell can you say that? You've only met her the one time."

"I could see it in her eyes when she looks at you." Barton took to whittling. "I may be old and alone, but I know when a woman is in love. And was fool enough to turn my back." He narrowed his eyes. "I'd hate for that to happen to you."

Zeke laughed. "If she's in love with me, how come she keeps turning me down when I ask her to marry me?"

"That's something the two of you will have to figure out."

"I know it's because of her mother filling her full of lies and her damn independent nature." He shot to his feet. "And I'm afraid that's going to get her killed before I can ask her to marry me, again."

Maeve was relieved, yet apprehensive when Cutter stopped the horses near a slow-running stream in the middle of a small willow-filled oasis. She wearily dismounted and stood next to the animal, giving her shaking legs a chance to register she wasn't sitting astride any longer. She'd sat horseback for the last twenty four hours with only the brief respite when they robbed the bank. Her legs wobbled like a newborn colt.

She sank to the ground, her tied hands resting in her lap. The coolness of the shaded area and the soft pallet of grass beneath her, beckoned. She straightened her legs out in front of her and slowly lowered her body to the cool ground. Closing her eyes, she extended her hands above her head and stretched. The pulling of muscles warmed her aching limbs, torso, and backside.

"Spread them legs and you'll be right where I want ya." Cutter's coarse comment sliced through her tranquility.

She sat up and glared at the man. "Touch me in that way and if I don't kill you, Zeke will." The harshness of her voice surprised her as much as it did the man standing over her. His eyes opened wide a moment, then slanted in a narrowed glare.

"Don't you go threatening me. I'm the one with the power. You're the one with her hands tied and mooning over a man who should have died trying to save you rather than cower to my demands."

So that was it. He thought Zeke a coward. She couldn't hold the laugh. Zeke was braver than this man who hid behind his gun. He thought he could win her over by ordering her around? As if that made him more of a man.

"What are you laughing at?" He grabbed her arm, hauling her to her feet.

She saw the gleam in Marsh's eyes. He was ready for Cutter to shoot her.

"I don't cower to anyone's demands. Not yours and not my husband's." She knew this man respected defiance. To him that was bravery. To her, at this moment, it could be the difference between seeing Zeke again and ending up with a bullet hole and dying right here.

A crooked smile played on the man's lips. "That's what I liked about you the first time we met. You've got spit." He ran a finger down her cheek. Her skin crawled. Her first reaction was to pull back, but that was what he expected.

She forced a smile and shook her head. "You can't touch me this way until I see my husband set free." She squelched the nausea rising at the look of desire that flamed in his eyes.

"You'd stay with me? And all I gotta do is set your husband loose?"

"Yes." Her knees nearly buckled at the deal she made with the vile man salivating as his gaze devoured her.

He didn't take his eyes off her as he motioned to Marsh. "You hear what she just said?" Cutter asked the other man.

"Yeah. I say she's playin' ya. Let's just shoot her and get back to divvy up the money." Marsh pointed his gun at her.

Cutter turned to the man. "I say she ain't." He pushed the gun aside. "If you shoot her before I find out, I'll ferget we're friends." The sinister undertone made her skin crawl.

Marsh shot her another one of his killer glares and stalked over to his horse. Cutter turned back to her. "How's about we test this deal." He stepped toward her. She didn't know what to do. But had no intention of giving herself to this man or even kissing him for that matter. Relief ebbed through her icy veins when he untied her hands.

"If you stay put while we sleep, I'll know you're not foolin' with me. If you take off—I'll let Jack hunt you down." The last sentence was said with no remorse. She was just a conquest should she stay. He could care less if she were dead or alive come morning. But if this worked, Zeke would be alive.

Chapter 18

Three riders rode down the opposite side of the canyon, but Maeve wasn't one of them. Zeke stalked back and forth. "What do you think they're going to do when they realize we're missing?" He turned to Barton, who sat nonchalantly whittling away. He didn't think the man even rolled up in his blanket to sleep. When Zeke dozed off and woke during the night the man sat there methodically whittling.

"I imagine the group that's down there right now won't do anything until Cutter or Marsh return." Barton glanced up at him. "That's one thing we learned early on about this bunch, none of the lackeys have a lick of brains between them. It's Cutter who has the smarts. Marsh would if he could get beyond his brother's death."

Zeke stared at the compound below them. Marsh was the biggest threat. Cutter could be bought or manipulated, but a man with revenge in his heart had only one mission—retribution.

"I hope Cutter has Maeve and not Marsh." Even as he stated it, he wished neither had her. A stick snapped behind him.

He froze.

Did the outlaws sneak up on them? They'd taken refuge on the west side of the compound believing the group would return from the east.

He reached down for his knife and glanced to see if Barton heard the noise. The man stood and smiled, extending his hand toward someone behind him. Damn. The man was in cahoots with the outlaws.

Zeke whipped around, he wasn't about to go down without finding Maeve. The hand holding the knife sliced through the air inches from his youngest brother's face.

"Dang, Zeke that's a heck of a way to great your brother." Gil's words might have been joking, but the grim set to his brother's mouth felt like someone cold cocked him again.

"How'd you find me? Is Maeve all right?" He dropped the knife and hugged his brother. Finally, someone he trusted.

Gil pulled out of the embrace. "Maeve told Darcy the outlaw's had you here." He wiped a hand across his weary face. "But I can't tell you where Maeve is. On my way to Boyd, I followed the tracks of nine horses. About two miles out of Monument they split into three groups. None of them headed straight this way. So I kept coming hoping to get here before the rest of them." He slapped Zeke on the back. "Looks like you don't need my help after all."

"This here's Barton. He's a Pinkerton."

"Pleased to meet you Marshal Halsey. Zeke didn't tell me he had a brother in law enforcement." Barton raised an eyebrow at Zeke.

"Didn't think it mattered. They have Maeve. Told me if I behaved they wouldn't kill her." He didn't want to think what they would do to her when they found him gone. "After they left with her, me and Barton got loose and tied up the man guarding us." He nodded his head to the man trussed up to a tree.

"Darcy said the man had a gun on Maeve and used her as a shield during the robbery." Gil stared beyond him. "Looks like another group coming in."

Zeke turned so fast, he nearly knocked Gil over. "Jacks and Jezebels. It's just more of the gang." His heart stopped. "Maeve is with Cutter and Marsh." Could Cutter save Maeve from Marsh? Would he even try?

"We need to be closer to the shacks when they arrive. If not, they could shoot Maeve as soon as they see I'm missing." Zeke picked his knife off the ground and slid it into the sheath in his boot.

"Let's even the odds, gentlemen." Barton stood, handing Gil a slingshot and keeping one for himself. The wood had been carved into a Y-shape, and he'd fastened what appeared to be portions of his suspenders to the Y. "These are quiet and all we need for ammunition are some small rocks."

Zeke looked at Gil and grinned. As boys they'd gotten in more trouble with slingshots than he wanted to count.

Barton and Gil found a pocket full of marble-sized rocks, and they all stealthily made their way down the side of the canyon to the buildings.

At the barn, Zeke whispered, "Let's each take a shack." He motioned Barton to the one on the left, Gil to the middle one, and he set out for the shack the farthest way. Peering in the window, he found all the returned outlaws playing cards and drinking whiskey. They weren't expecting anyone to sneak into camp, least of all the men who'd escaped.

He leaned against the building. Storming the place with one gun and slingshots wasn't a good idea. They'd just have to wait until the outlaws came out one at a time to relieve themselves. When Gil and Barton joined him, they both agreed and took spots where they could keep an eye on who returned and the men in the shack.

Zeke had barely found his spot when a man stumbled out the door and headed to the corner of the shack. Barton nailed him in the head with a stone. The man went down with his dick hanging out. Zeke grinned as he helped Gil drag the man to the other shack. They gagged and tied him up before heading back to their hiding spots.

By the fourth man down, he began to wonder about the remaining men. Didn't they think it strange their cohorts hadn't returned? When the next to last man came out, Gil hit him, knocking the man to the ground, and Zeke entered the shack. The remaining outlaw was so drunk he wasn't even scared.

"Hey, you're the guy I knocked out. I didn't think you'd go down so easy." The man laughed, and Zeke knocked out two of his teeth before his fist sunk in the man's gut. He hauled the moaning man to the building housing all the outlaws.

"He put up a fight?" Gil asked, gawking at the

blood spurting out the man's mouth.

"Nope." Zeke shoved the man onto a chair and started wrapping him with rope.

"You just beat him up because you felt like it?" Gil crossed his arms and stared at Zeke.

"Yeah. He's the one who cold cocked me when I tried to see where Cutter took Maeve."

"So he deserved it." Gil watched him like a disapproving old woman.

"Yeah, and it felt good. So stop being a goody-goody lawman and think like a brother." Zeke stood and faced him. Gil might be the law, but he'd still whip his ass if the need arose.

"Boys, we need to make a plan for the return of Cutter, Marsh, and Miss Loman." Barton stood at the window peering through the burlap curtains.

Maeve's stiff body refused to uncurl when the toe of a boot jabbed her in the backside. "We'll be back to your husband by the end of the day if you get up and get moving." Cutter's words sent her heart fluttering. She wanted to see Zeke. It was all that kept her from fleeing during the night. That and the fact she didn't have a clue which way to go to escape the men watching her. One like a ravenous wolf, and the other like a deadly rattler.

She pushed into a sitting position, raising her body off the cold, hard ground and held back a whimper. Her stiff legs didn't want to move.

"Come on, we ain't got all day." Marsh grabbed her arm, jerking her to her feet. Her legs buckled, and Marsh drew his gun, pointing it at her head.

"Go ahead. Put me out of my misery." She

stared up the barrel. "You're just going to shoot Zeke the minute you see him anyway and then me. Why not just get it over with." She'd thought about it all night. There was no way they were going to let either of them go. All she could hope for was Gil found Zeke and they got away or he would find their bodies and give Zeke a proper burial.

"Put that thing away!" Cutter grabbed the pistol and back-handed Marsh, knocking the smaller man on his backside. "You aren't going to shoot her. Least ways not until I've had some fun."

He wasn't keeping her alive because he cared. She knew better. He planned to have his way with her. She cringed, knowing she'd rather take a bullet than bare her body to the man. But she had to stay alive until they returned to the ranch. She had to know if Zeke got away. Then she'd shoot herself before she'd let the man touch her intimately.

Cutter took hold of her arms, drawing her up off her knees. He dipped his head, and she raised a hand, placing it over his lips. "I said I won't carry on with you until Zeke is free. If you kill him or don't set him free, you won't get anything." She peered into his eyes, "And if you force me without doing as I ask, I'll kill you."

"You threatening me?" he growled, grasping her hands and pulling them down to her side as he leaned in to press his lips to hers.

She thrust her knee into his groin as hard as she could and backed away before he hit her in the head as he doubled over.

"You bitch! I should kill you now!" Cutter clutched between his legs and writhed on the ground. Marsh stood by the horses grinning like a man with a fist full of money.

Maeve strolled to her horse and mounted. She walked her horse up next to Cutter. "I said on my terms. If you want me warm and willing that's the way it will be." She motioned for Marsh to lead the way and fell in behind his horse. It was some time before she heard Cutter's horse trotting up behind her.

She sat tall in the saddle as her insides churned and her heart pounded like a runaway horse. Maiming his manhood was a low thing to any man. She wasn't sure Cutter would be willing to wait her out now that she'd harmed him. For all she knew he'd point a gun at her and leave her alongside the trail.

"You do that to me again and I won't spare you from Marsh," Cutter said, riding even with her horse.

She nodded. "Then don't push your affections on me until my husband is free. I won't give myself to anyone until I know he's safe."

"How do I know he won't come back after you?" He narrowed his eyes. "How do I know you don't have something set up where you'll do me in and return to him?"

"I only want Zeke safe. I'll do whatever it takes to make him leave." Her heart ached at the thought of what she would have to do and tell him to get him to leave. He'd been so persistent for better than a year to get her to love him and marry him. She bit down on her bottom lip to stop the tears forming. She'd fallen hard for him. He'd shown her commitment, love, and acceptance of her past and her father's past. She hiccupped, holding back the tears. She loved him and needed him.

Maeve jerked her horse to a stop. She didn't need anyone. Cutter booted her horse in the rump, the animal jumped forward with her clinging to the saddle horn. To be in Zeke's strong arms right now and know he would get her out of this—she did need him. And not just to get her out of this mess. She needed his strength to learn to trust.

These thoughts banged around in her head as they kept a steady trot-walk pattern all day and into the late afternoon.

Marsh stopped at the opening of a valley. Maeve looked beyond him and spotted the shacks and barn. Her stomach tightened. She'd soon know if she and Zeke would get out of this alive.

"Somethin's not right." Marsh stared at the buildings. "There's no one moving about. Everyone else should have made it back by now." He shifted his gaze to the horses and counted out loud. "All the horses are here."

Cutter grabbed the reins of her horse. "Let's split up. You head in from the east, I'll take the south."

Marsh nodded and moved into the trees, heading toward the buildings from the back. Cutter led her horse into the trees in the opposite direction. His gaze never left the buildings as he maneuvered the horses in behind the barn.

He dismounted and pulled her down off the horse. "You don't go shoutin' or I'll have to shut you up." He pointed his pistol at her head. The click of the hammer as he cocked the gun made her flinch.

She gulped and nodded. He grasped her hand

so hard pain shot through her fingers, and she stifled a cry. Cutter set off in a crouch toward the first building. He peered into the window and moved to the next shack.

He hissed out a breath and leaned against the building. "I think your husband is waiting for us."

The sound of a rifle cocking reverberated in the air around them.

"You're right, I am." The sound of Zeke's voice wrenched a sob from her chest.

Cutter wrapped an arm around her before she could think about running into Zeke's strong arms. "Remember our deal? You're gonna be my outlaw in petticoats." He said, placing his lips much too intimately against her cheek.

Zeke's eyes narrowed and his lips formed a straight disapproving line. She wondered if the outlaw would hold to the deal. Was it worth hurting Zeke to find out?

"Tell him. Tell him you're gonna stay with me." Cutter squeezed her and she squeaked.

Zeke stepped forward. She put her hand up as Cutter clicked the hammer back on his pistol. Who would shoot first? Most likely Cutter since he held her in front of him. Zeke would have to take a chance on hitting her should he shoot.

She had to stall. There was still a chance Zeke could take him without getting hurt.

"Zeke, I'm staying with Cutter."

"I don't believe you." The gun in Zeke's hand faltered slightly as he tore his gaze from her face to the man cupping her breast.

Her throat tightened with revulsion. She wanted to shout at Zeke to shoot the disgusting man, but they'd both die. She had to believe Cutter would let him go.

Gulping down the bile and fear clogging her throat, she placed her hands on either side of Cutter's face. She didn't dare look at Zeke. Not if she planned to be convincing. Her heart bled with regret, and she fought her body's revulsion as she lowered her lips and kissed the vile outlaw.

<h1 style="text-align:center">Chapter 19</h1>

"No!" Zeke couldn't believe the sight before him—Maeve kissing a man who fondled her as if she were a whore. His heart ripped in two. "You don't mean this."

He dropped the gun to his side and walked toward them. If he could just touch her, get her out of that man's arms. Cutter's gun came up, only this time the barrel pointed at Maeve.

"She and I made a deal. She's mine and you leave. Now!" Cutter pulled back the hammer and placed the end of the barrel against Maeve's heaving sides.

Zeke sought her face. Her eyes pleaded with him. For what? To save her or to leave? There was no way in two days time she could have fallen in love with Cutter. Love meant trust. She wouldn't have trusted him as far as she could toss him.

Her eyes glistened with unshed tears. She made the deal with Cutter to save him. The realization nearly brought him to his knees. He'd worked so hard to get her to accept his love. And now she'd given the ultimate sacrifice.

Where the hell were Gil and Barton? He growled and took a step backwards. There was no way in hell he'd leave Maeve to that man. He didn't care if she did kiss Cutter and allowed his hands all over her, her eyes said otherwise—she needed him.

He dropped the rifle on the ground. "She's all yours. I only said we were married to save her hide. Now I see how fickle she is." His heart squeezed when she flinched at his words. If Maeve believed him, and he could get Cutter to think he didn't care what happened to her, he might have a chance of getting her away from the outlaw. He'd have to harness his anger and revulsion at the man and love for the woman to make it happen.

"You really ain't married?" Cutter looked at Maeve. Zeke caught a glimpse of someone at the corner of the building. He hoped it was Gil.

Maeve shook her head and croaked, "No. We aren't really married."

He kept his gaze locked on the two in front of him to not give away his brother sneaking up behind Cutter and Maeve.

"She cooked up the idea of us being married," Zeke continued to keep the outlaw's attention.

"Your idea?" Cutter looked at Maeve. The leer and satisfaction in the man's voice made Zeke's teeth grind. He needed to keep the man's eyes forward.

"Yeah, makes me wonder what other schemes she's been cooking up." That snapped the outlaw's gaze back to him. The outlaw's gun wobbled, and his grip loosened on Maeve.

Gil grabbed Maeve, throwing her to the ground. In one fluid motion, Zeke pulled the knife from his boot, hurled it toward the outlaw, and dropped, rolling to the side. He'd preformed this act more times than he cared to remember while helping Gil.

Cutter fired. The bullet whizzed through the air where Zeke had stood. The second shot went into the ground before the gun dropped from Cutter's hand, and he clutched the knife protruding from the middle of his chest.

Crawling on his hands and knees, Zeke hurried to Maeve. Gil rose off the woman and attended the wide-eyed outlaw. Zeke pulled her into his arms, clutching her to his pounding heart.

"You're safe. Shh." He pushed back loose strands of hair and kissed her forehead. Her tear-rimmed, beautiful, blue eyes held his gaze. "I've been so worried about you. And when he..." Zeke studied her face. Her quivering lips and shaking hands did little to settle his nerves.

"I-I only told him t-that and k-kissed him so he would let you go. Please don't hate me." She bit her bottom lip as tears streamed down her cheeks.

"I know you only did it to protect me. There's no way you would fall for someone that easily. Shucks, look how long it's taken me to get you to care whether I live or die." He smiled, trying to reassure her.

She scrubbed the back of her hand across her lips.

"Here let me help." He dipped his head. There was one way to take away the reminder of what she'd done. He covered her mouth with his, seducing her lips. Slowly, she relaxed in his arms and returned the kiss with enthusiasm.

"Ahem. We're still missing one." Gil's voice broke into his euphoria.

He continued to hold Maeve as he looked up at his smirking brother. "Well, what are you doing standing around here, go find him."

"I'm not leaving you two sitting here in the open not paying attention to anything but each other." Gil toed Zeke in the backside. "Get up and at least get in a building."

Growling, Zeke glared at Gil and stood, pulling Maeve up beside him.

Barton appeared. "Marsh high-tailed it when shots were fired." He spotted Maeve and stepped forward. "Do you mind?" he asked and folded Maeve into a hug without waiting for an answer. "Young woman, you are truly your father's daughter!"

Maeve pulled out of his embrace. Was that a compliment? She stared at the man and looked at Zeke beaming like a proud parent. What was going on?

"What do you mean? I thought my father was an outlaw, how can I be like him, unless you mean because I participated in a robbery." She glared at the man. "And I surely don't see that as being something to be proud of."

"We've got a lot to tell you." Zeke grasped her hand and pulled her protectively against his side. Instead of pulling away, as she would have a month ago, she snuggled into him. He'd proven he would never leave her, even when faced with the worse.

"What do you have to tell me?" She wrapped her arms around Zeke. His solid body and warmth gave her a sense of strength and home.

"It's too late today to take these men and money back to Monument." Gil motioned toward Cutter's dead body and a shack. "Let's find some food and these two can fill us both in on your pa."

"That's an excellent idea." Barton motioned to follow him. He set out at a brisk pace for the building on the far end.

She leaned into Zeke. "I take it what he has to say is good news?"

"Yes and no. Yes, your pa wasn't an outlaw, but he is dead." Zeke squeezed her. "I'm sorry."

Tears didn't come. She knew he was dead. That was one thing Cutter said that she believed. If Jack Marsh got his hands on her father, she didn't doubt for one minute the man had killed him. She peered behind her at the tree-dotted canyon walls. He wouldn't be happy until she was dead as well.

She squared her shoulders. That was fine with her. When he came looking for her, she'd take an eye for an eye.

They'd finished a meal of biscuits, made by Barton, and salt pork, which Gil had scrounged up. Maeve looked around the table at each of the men grinning at her.

"My pa was a Pinkerton? A man who enforced the law?" She still couldn't believe it, even though it fit the image she remembered of him. She clutched Zeke's hand. "He would have come back to us if Marsh hadn't killed him."

"Yes, just like his letter said. He didn't run out on you and your mother, and he wasn't a miner," Zeke said pointedly and raised an eyebrow.

"So you can't hold that against my brother any longer," Gil said, leaning back in his chair and stretching his legs.

"How's Darcy? When is the baby due?" She was glad Darcy had kept a level head when she realized who Maeve was and gave her message to Gil so quickly.

"She's fine. I wish she was more like normal women." He frowned.

"How so?" She knew when Gil met Darcy he thought she was a young man, but she didn't understand his consternation about her being with child.

"She insisted on going with me to Monument to deliver a prisoner. Told me if I left her behind, she'd just follow me."

Zeke slapped Gil on the back. "You should be used to that by now."

"I thought with her condition and all, she'd quiet down some, but she seems to be worse!"

Maeve caught Zeke staring at her. "What?"

"Just wondered if you'd be as contrary when you're in the same condition."

Her face heated, and her insides quivered. What would it be like to carry this man's child?

"I'm gonna go check the prisoners and then me and Barton will bunk in the next shack over and take turns keeping an eye on them." Gil stood, tipping his tin cup and swallowing the last drop.

Barton stood. "I'll go with you." He extended

his hand to her. "I am most happy you're back with us Miss Loman."

"Thank you. Please call me Maeve."

Barton smiled and left the shack behind Gil. She stood to clean the table. An arm looped around her waist, and she landed on Zeke's lap.

"Those can wait." The expression on his face and the heat in his eyes made her shiver with anticipation. His lips claimed hers, and she forgot everything—her pa, Cutter, her need for independence. She wanted to bask in the notion this man could make her happy. Tilting her head back, she gave him access to the sensitive skin under her chin.

"I have an idea." His words vibrated against her neck, making her lower region ripple in response.

"What." Her mouth was so dry the word came out as a bark.

"I'm going to get some buckets of water, and then I'm going to wash all the trail dust off of you."

She snapped out of the languid trance. "I'm sorry. I didn't—" Zeke placed a finger on her lips.

"Just pull the curtains and wait for me." He stood, placing her on her feet beside the table. Zeke flashed a devilish grin and disappeared out the door with three buckets.

The door closed, and she hurried to close the curtains on the one window. She returned to the middle of the room. The shack housed a table and chairs, potbellied stove, and two narrow beds built against the wall. The walls could use some mud caulking, the last rays of sun slanted through the boards. Should she disrobe waiting for him? But what if someone came in, like Marsh? A shudder chilled her at the thought of the man finding her naked. No, she'd wait for Zeke. He'd protect her.

The door banged open. Standing in the doorway, carrying three buckets slopping over with water was a man she would forever hold dear. He grinned from ear to ear as he placed the buckets on the floor and turned to secure the door.

Contentment washed through her as she watched his broad back. This man would never leave her. Never make her feel unwanted.

He faced her. His emotions illuminated his face and burned in his eyes. Like a cougar, he stalked across the room.

"Do you want your bath warm or cold?" His husky voice made her stomach quiver.

"I don't think either one of us has the patience to start a fire and warm the water." She began unbuttoning her blouse.

Zeke licked his lips as his gaze locked on her long fingers slowly, seductively, opening her blouse. He ached with want.

Clearing his throat, he said, "Keep getting out of them clothes." Then turned to put his hat on a peg by the door and place a bucket of water on the table. He hunted around the room for a cloth, but couldn't find one.

A soft thud brought his gaze back to Maeve. She stood by the table in the lacy underclothes he'd bought her. It seemed like a year since he'd ventured into that dress shop.

"I can't find a cloth to wash you with." His breath caught as she grasped his large hands in her long, slender ones.

"Your hands will do just fine." Maeve peeled the chemise over her head, rolled the drawers down to the floor, and stepped out of them. She stood before him like an alabaster figurine. A shy, yet, come-hither smile enticed him and released his pent-up passion.

They had all night, and he intended to use every minute of it showing her what she meant to him. "Sit." He pointed to the chair next to the bucket and table.

Without hesitating she sat. Zeke glanced around the room and found a sizeable kettle by the stove. He placed the kettle behind the chair and tilted her head back. With great care, he untied the rawhide holding her hair in a braid and worked the twined strands loose. Her dark mane fell in waves toward the kettle.

Maeve slid her bottom to the edge of the seat, lowering her head to rest on the back of the chair. He gawked at her long, white, reclining body. Her stomach muscles fluttered, and her legs spread slightly to keep her on the seat. His cock strained at the buttons on his Levis.

Zeke inhaled, bringing his gaze back to her hair. He raised the bucket and poured.

"Oh!" Maeve nearly shot out of the chair. "That's colder than I expected." Her rosy nipples puckered and her stomach sunk as she sucked in air.

"Sorry, do you want me to heat it up?" He wanted to rest his hand on the dark hair at the juncture of her legs and suckle the tantalizing breasts.

"No. I'm ready for it now," she said in a whisper. He worked his hands through her soft hair, scrubbing her head and watching the rapid rise and fall of her chest as she breathed. He poured more water on her hair and twisted the strands to wring the water out.

"Close your eyes," he whispered close to her ear and dipped his hands in the bucket. Drizzling water onto her forehead, he watched the rivulets make tracks in the dust on her face. He scooped more, washing the dust from her peaceful face and on down her neck to her shoulders and chest. He used his hands to push the dirt and water down her skin. The dirt floor became a puddle, but he didn't care. All that mattered was Maeve's silky, hot skin under his hands.

Maeve sighed as the spot between her legs throbbed with each inch Zeke's hands washed and caressed her body.

"Stand." The one word broke into her lethargic haze.

Zeke held out his hand, helping her to her feet. He stood her over the kettle and slowly poured water down her body. It splashed around her feet, making the floor muddy. He placed the empty bucket on the floor and carried the kettle of dirty water to the door.

"Now, it's my turn." He stood by the chair, undressing. She couldn't take her eyes off him as he revealed his tantalizing body, button-by-button. He tossed his shirt to the side, shoved the top of his long johns down to his waist, and sat on the chair, pulling off his boots and socks.

She ran her hands over his muscled shoulders and down his back. The thought of running her hands all over his body as he had hers made her quake and burn.

He shucked his pants and drawers and sat in the chair his legs sprawled and all his male glory rising toward the ceiling. She wanted to wash that magnificent appendage first, but knew she should start at the top and work her way down.

She used a cup to dip and pour water on Zeke's head. She worked her fingers through his curls and massaged his head watching his lips curve in satisfaction as his maleness became thicker.

Drizzling water over his face, she used her hands to push the water and dirt from his scratchy stubble of whiskers. Her fingers stopped on his lips. The contrast of the rough bristles against the pads of her fingers and then his soft, supple lips sent tendrils of heat swirling in her belly. What would it feel like on her lips?

She bent, gently rubbing her lips across the whiskers on his cheek, then touched his lips. The sensation made her wet between her legs. She straightened and stared at Zeke. His open eyes watched her.

"What's wrong?" he asked, putting a hand on her hip. The connection of his calloused hand on her skin started another jolt of sensations coursing through her.

Her whole body hummed. "I'm..." she touched the spot between her legs and brought her hand up. Her fingers were slick.

A smile as broad as his face lit up his eyes. "Hurry this bath along, so I can relieve your problem."

She picked up a bucket and poured it slowly

down his body. His maleness became less rigid, but by the time she'd wiped him all down and stood him to rinse his back, it was evident Zeke was more than ready to fulfill her desires.

He swept her into his arms and carried her to one of the beds. "When I realized Marsh and Cutter took you, it was all Barton could to do make me see waiting for your return was the best option." He placed her on the bed. "Tonight, I want to show you what you mean to me."

"And I will show you," she purred and took him in her hands.

"Oh Lord! Don't do that or I can't promise you any fun."

Maeve laughed. She loved the fact she had that kind of power over the large man. Cutter had fallen for wiles she didn't know she had and showed her the kind of power a woman possessed, if she used it right. And watched herself. With the man looming over her, she wanted to use her powers to bring him pleasure he'd never dreamed of.

Zeke's arms circled her body, crushing her breasts against his hard chest. His rigid length pressed between her legs as he kissed her breathless.

Chapter 20

Stars filled Maeve's head. Her body shook from the surge of heat and sensations. Just when she thought the miracle was over, her body tightened and sparks shot to her fingers and toes, exploding from where Zeke filled her. She bit his shoulder and clung to him with claw-like hands as the wave washed over her.

"I wanted to show you a good time," she panted as another wave of sensations warmed her body.

"Sweetheart, believe me, you are." Zeke suckled her breast and waited. It would be dawn before long, and he knew his brother wouldn't want to waste any daylight. The night had been full of passion and little sleep. He wasn't complaining.

"Watch me." He rose up on his hands on either side of her head and slowly entered and retreated. She licked her lips and writhed under him, her hips pressing upward, taking him in to the hilt.

Her eyes glazed over and her breathing came

in pants. He held on just long enough to explode at the same time she convulsed around him. He growled. His body went limp, and he collapsed on Maeve, seizing her lips and demonstrating his emotions for her.

She turned her head, gasping for air. "Please, can't breathe."

"Sorry," he rolled to the side, gathering her in his arms. Kissing the top of her head, he held her tight. He didn't want to spend another night without her in his arms. "After we help Gil get the outlaws to Monument, we'll go to Baker City, tell your ma about your pa and then how about a wedding?"

She stiffened in his arms. Was she still going to fight him on marriage?

"I was thinking more along the lines of helping Gil and going back to McEwen and teaching school." He heard the anxiety in her voice.

"You don't plan to tell your ma about your pa?" He'd start there and work his way to the marriage question.

"I think she knew what he did and kept it from me only to keep me disillusioned. I'll not go back and question her. I'm sure it will only bring me more pain since that's what she likes to inflict upon me."

Zeke turned Maeve to face him. He wrapped his arms around her, drawing her soft curves against him. "She can't hurt you anymore. You know the truth. I think you've felt it in your heart the whole time." He kissed her. "Your father loved you. He wouldn't have left you voluntarily." He kissed her again, longer, deeper. "And I love you and won't leave you."

She sighed and snuggled her head against his chest. "I know," she whispered.

"Then why don't you want to marry me?" He pulled back to scan her face.

"It's not that I don't want to marry you. I love being in your arms and feeling your strength. It's- well- I don't want to lose my independence." She stared him full in the face, defying him to say something.

Zeke knew how important that independence was to her. He laughed. "Woman, you think I don't know that? I'd never stifle your independence. If you want to go back to teaching I don't care as long as you're in my bed at night and there to discuss things. Shucks, if you want to run for mayor, I'll vote for you and help you campaign." He cuddled her close. "I just don't want to lose you."

Her arms twined around his neck. "I'll try not to get lost." Maeve's lips caressed his, and he was lost in the feel and taste of her.

"Sun's peekin' over the canyon wall, time to go!" Gil shouted and banged on the door.

Maeve jumped and Zeke laughed. "We'll be out shortly."

"Barton's got coffee and biscuits. But if you aren't out soon, you'll go without."

"Guess we better get dressed or get left behind." He gave Maeve one more squeeze and let her roll to the side of the bed. When she stood, he couldn't resist smacking her pretty, little backside.

"Hey!" She jumped away from the bed and wiggled the delightful package as she bent to retrieve her drawers off the floor. The sight made him stiff and he groaned. Maeve grinned at him over her shoulder and he laughed. The little flirt knew what she'd done.

"Tame that animal and get dressed," she said, tossing his flannels to him.

He smiled and dressed, watching her and raising his eyebrow when she glanced his way. He loved the playfulness that had emerged. This was the feisty woman he knew lurked under her unexpressive teacher's mask. They managed to get dressed quickly and set off to the other shack for food. His stomach growled. He'd worked up an appetite with all the activity during the night. Maeve's belly growled, too. He glanced over at her. The cute smile playing on her lips was more than he could resist.

He pulled her into his arms, kissing the up-turned corners of her mouth before taking full control.

"I hope you two get hitched soon," Gil said from behind them.

Zeke raised his head and grinned. "I'm afraid being married isn't going to make me want her any less."

Maeve blushed and slid from his arms. He watched her hurry to the shack.

"She going to marry you?" The worried tone in Gil's voice didn't escape Zeke.

"I hope so. We're still working it out." He knew it would be a matter of showing to Maeve she wasn't losing anything and only gaining by getting married.

"The news about her father should've helped." Gil started toward the shack.

"It did, but she's still got a notion being married will take away her independence."

Gil snorted. "She needs to have a talk with my wife. I swear she's the most independent female a person could come across."

"Good Idea. I'll bring her by your place when we get through in Monument." He smiled. Yes, a good dose of Darcy would show Maeve being married didn't take away any of her independence.

They'd been on the trail several hours when sitting in the saddle became unbearable for Maeve. She and Zeke had made love several times during the night. She'd never forget how wonderful it all was, but her lower regions couldn't take another minute in the saddle. Expecially after the torturous ride with the outlaws.

Gil and Zeke rode at the head of the line of outlaws tied to their horses. Zeke led the horse Cutter's body was thrown over. Barton rode in the back with her. He'd regaled her with stories about the Pinkerton's and some of her father's jobs with the agency.

The horses splashed through a small stream. A grove of cottonwood trees dotted the area and spread away from the stream. "I need to stop. You go on, I'll catch up." She reined in her horse and hopped out of the saddle.

"Let me ride up and tell the others." Barton urged his horse forward before she could tell him it wasn't necessary.

Maeve put her hand on her pistol. Strapping the holster back on her hips this morning helped her gain normalcy after the last few days. She tied her horse to a tree, letting it graze while she stretched her back and willed the dull throb between her legs to ease. She wished it was the sensation Zeke brought instead of the ache brought on by the constant rocking in the saddle.

The group ahead had rounded a bend. Good. A few moments to herself. She found a spot behind a cloying bitterbrush bush to answer the call of nature. She studied the small, yellow flowers on the bush and tried to hold her breath. The sickly sweet scent of the flower made her nauseous.

She stood and hurried back to her horse. Just as Zeke rounded the bend a rope looped over her, capturing her arms against her body before a hand clasped her mouth. She struggled, but the rope remained tight around her arms, hindering her use of them. Maeve dug in her heels as someone dragged her backward into the denser trees and brush. From the height of the person, she knew her assailant. Jack Marsh.

"Quiet or I'll put a bullet through your man." His breath opposite of the bitterbush was just as nauseating.

She tried to stomp on his toes, but he kept his feet well out of reach. Her hand touched the butt of her gun. She couldn't shoot him, but she'd warn Zeke. The barrel barely slipped from the holster before she pulled the trigger.

At the shot Zeke raced his horse forward. He couldn't be killed, not now. She wiggled and stomped to keep Marsh from getting a good aim at Zeke. His hand slid from her mouth.

"Stop!" she screamed and wrenched out of

Marsh's grip. Facing the man, she raised the pistol the best she could with a rope anchoring her arm to her side. Marsh curled his lip in a sneer and aimed the gun at Zeke still riding like his horse's tail was on fire.

"No!" She pulled the trigger shooting the gun from Marsh's hand. He yelped and tugged on the rope around her, knocking the pistol out of her grasp. She dropped to her knees in an attempt to reclaim the weapon.

"I'll show you." Marsh jumped on a horse and wrapped the rope around the saddle horn. Jabbing the horse in the ribs, he pulled her onto her back and took off dragging her through the trees and brush.

Maeve grabbed the rope and tried to hold her back up off the ground, allowing the heavier material of her riding skirt to slide along the ground. The speed at which she traveled frightened her as much as the ground, rocks, and sticks battering her body. She stared back the way they'd come.

Tears blurred her vision of Zeke. He'd stopped his horse.

Why didn't he pursue and stop the crazed man? Something solid struck her in the back, she winced and tried to keep her eyes on Zeke, but soon lost sight of him in the trees. Marsh continued for over a mile dragging her and cussing. Every time he swerved, her body rammed into a rock or was sliced by sticks and thorny bushes. The man was trying to drag her to death.

Her body trembled from the effort of keeping her head from hitting a rock. She couldn't take much more. Where was Zeke? He could have easily caught up to them by now. Why did he stop? It was pretty clear—for all his talk—she was the only person she could trust to get her away from this maniac. Or die alone—just like her father.

Zeke stared at the lunatic dragging the woman he loved through the trees. Every muscle in his body wanted to charge forward, but to follow would only cause Maeve more harm. His throat burned with the need to scream his frustration. He'd not give the man that satisfaction. He took a deep breath, calculated the direction Marsh was headed, and reined in his emotions. He needed a clear head if he were to outthink and outmaneuver the man dragging the woman he loved. Taking a deep breath, he turned his attention to Maeve's horse. He leaned down and untied it from a tree. She'd need the animal when he found her.

He scanned the area, noting with a grimace the easy to follow trail of Maeve's towed body. Something shiny glinted as the limbs of the trees moved in the slight breeze. He urged his horse to the spot.

Maeve's pistol.

He dismounted, picking up the gun. The warm steel and faint gun powder scent eased his thoughts some. It was Maeve's shots, he'd heard. She could have wounded the bastard. If so, her odds of getting free multiplied.

The vision of her being pulled through the trees flashed. Damn, the man that did this to her. He shoved the weapon in his saddlebag and re-mounted.

"Zeke, wait!" Barton rode up alongside of him both his horse and himself out of breath.

"Go back and help Gil get those men to the authorities." Zeke looped a rope around Maeve's mare and then fastened the rope to his saddle horn.

"Where's Maeve?" the older man questioned, staring at the riderless horse.

"Marsh has her." He nearly bit through his cheek as he held back the oath and anxiety burning in his throat. No sense getting this man all worked up. Gil needed his helped.

"Which way did they go?" Barton scanned the area. His brows formed one continuous line when he noticed the wide area of flattened plants. "That looks like—"

"Yep. That's why I'm taking my time. If he isn't being followed he won't drag her as far." I hope.

Barton peered at him. "You've got better nerves than I would if my lady was being hauled behind a horse like a downed log."

"The only thing keeping me here is knowing it's best to keep my distance until I find them, then sneak in. Alone." He stared at the man pointedly.

"I agree. I'll go help Gil. We'll wait for you and Maeve in Monument." Barton put a hand on his shoulder. "Marsh isn't fit to live."

Zeke nodded and Barton turned his horse. When the sound of hooves faded, he took a deep breath and urged his horse forward. If he was lucky, Marsh would have stopped by now and hopefully either be planning his next move, or at the very least, put Maeve on the horse with him.

Maeve lay on the ground curled in a ball. He'd finally stopped. She ached all over from her head, which had taken some blows, to her toes clenching in her boots. She'd known when something worse was going to happen. Marsh would cackle, and she'd hit a rock or be dragged over a thorny bush or log with protruding limbs.

It didn't feel like any bones broke, but her back burned from raw skin, cuts, and bruises. Something trickled down her head. Where was Zeke? She needed him. Wanted him. Where were his strong arms to cradle her and ease the pain? And oh God, the pain... Nothing could hurt this intense.

"You ain't such a tough female now are ya?" Marsh stepped up to her. His wide eyes glanced about frantically. He leaned down, grasping the rope and pulling her to a sitting position. Maeve cringed and hated herself for showing fear.

"Come on, you're gonna wait right here for that man to come get you." He hoisted her to her feet. "Then I'll take care of both of you and not be looking over my shoulder no more." Marsh tossed the rope over a tree limb and hoisted her up with her feet barely touching the ground. When he stepped close, she tried to kick him, but her leg didn't cooperate. Her body just swung back and forth working the rope tighter about her arms and body.

She wanted to cry out in pain and frustration, but she'd rather die than give the man the satisfaction of knowing he'd reduced her to a blubbering mass of hysteria.

"Zeke won't come after me." She smiled as he

stared at her.

"I seen the way he carries after you. He'll be here." Marsh walked to his tied horse and pulled hardtack out of his saddlebag.

"He won't. No one cares enough about me to give a hoot what you do." As she said the words the vision of Zeke sitting on his horse watching, as this lunatic towed her away brought on a despair worse than when her mother told her Pa was dead. Did she love Zeke more than her father? There it was. The word she'd tried so hard to hedge around. Love. She'd told herself years ago, she'd never love anyone. It hurt too much when they left.

Yet, here she was about to die and all she wanted was to tell Zeke she loved him. Tears burned her eyes. She gulped air to keep from sobbing. He abandoned her—and she still loved him.

Just like her father.

Chapter 21

Zeke spotted Maeve and Marsh. He turned to the right, moving farther away from the two, circling around to approach from the opposite side. When he was comfortable with the distance between his horses and his objective, he slid off and tied the two.

He slipped through the cover of brush and trees silently. Maeve's sagging body suspended from a tree stopped his heart. Damn the man! He'd be more than happy to carve Marsh into a million pieces. Shaking his head to clear away the haze of rage, he stared at the woman he loved to determine not only how bad her injuries, but how to get her away.

Maeve moved her head. Tears washed a clean path down her dirty face. His blood boiled with anger. He wanted to wrap his hands around the man's throat and not let go until Marsh hung limp. He'd never seen her look so lost and helpless. The sight ripped at his heart and twisted his gut.

It wasn't something he'd forget. Where was the strength he loved about her?

Skimming her body with his gaze, he noticed the blood, cuts, and bruises through her shredded blouse. He grasped a tree to keep from hurtling his body onto the man sitting on the stump, watching the opposite direction. He had to take his time. If he rushed in, Marsh could shoot Maeve before he could take him down. He had to get the man's attention focused toward him.

To step out in full view would put a bullet in him. He glanced at Maeve. Her dangling from the tree made it hard for him to concentrate on a foolproof plan. Maybe he should get her free then concentrate on Marsh? But to free her would make them easy targets.

He scanned the tree and how the rope was tied.

Marsh stood.

Zeke stepped back behind a tree, keeping his gaze trained on the outlaw. The man surveyed the area, and with one hand holding his rifle, he unbuttoned his pants. Not even turning his back to Maeve—he peed.

Now. Zeke burst from hiding and hit the man from behind, knocking him to the ground. Being larger, he straddled Marsh, shoving his face in the dirt with one hand and pushing the rifle away with the other.

"Mmph!"

He jerked the man's hands behind his back and looked around for something to bind them. Zeke held Marsh's arms behind his back, using the technique he'd picked up from Barton, and yanked him to his feet.

"Ow!" hollered Marsh.

"What's a matter can't take what you give out?" He propelled Marsh toward the horse and used the reins to tie the man's hands behind his back. Once he was secured, Zeke hurried to Maeve.

He slipped his knife out and cut the rope, dropping her into his arms. Holding her with one arm, he carefully removed the rope from around her body. His fingers dipped into the indentions the cord made and touched the sticky blood oozing from her wounds.

Zeke glared at the man sulking by the horse. It took all his willpower to not walk over and plunge his knife into the deserving man and twist.

"You came." The whispered disbelief shattered his heart.

"I'll always come for you," he said, lifting her into his arms.

"Ow!" The pain in her cry sliced through Zeke. He placed her on the ground in a bed of soft grass. She rolled to her side, and he witnessed the injuries to her back up close.

He rose, walked over to Marsh, and punched the man in the face as hard as he could. Marsh's head snapped back, and his knees buckled. Zeke didn't bother making sure the man was out of the way of the nervous horse's hooves as he retrieved the canteen from the saddle horn and returned to Maeve.

"I want you to lean against me." The pain in her eyes made him hanker to go back and inflict more pain on the man moaning behind him. He helped Maeve to her knees, facing him. He tucked her against his chest and used his knife to cut the torn remnants of her blouse and chemise away from her gashed, scraped, and bruised back. Her sharp hiss as he picked the pieces of fabric out of her wounds ripped at his insides. He hated her pain. Hated the fact he couldn't save her from Marsh and Cutter before him.

Satisfied he'd gotten it all, he leaned back. "Sit up a moment." He unbuttoned his shirt, pulling the tails out of his trousers. With his knife, he cut the bottom off the shirt and doused it with water. "This'll hurt, but I need to clean those cuts."

Maeve leaned forward, placing her hands on his muscular shoulders clad in the familiar red-flannel drawers. She nuzzled the unfastened buttons apart and rested her cheek against his warm, solid chest. If not for the pain from her wounds she would be in heaven, leaning against his strong form and inhaling his masculine scent.

A tear slid down her cheek, slipping between her face and his chest. He came for her. She ran his words over in her head. "I'll always come for you." He'd proven that over and over, again. Her heart had known he would come. It was her stubborn head that insisted she didn't need his help or anyone's.

She clutched his shoulders as he dug into a cut.

"Sorry. That one is deep and has a lot of dirt in it." The crack in his voice sounded as though he held back tears. "I need more water. Our horses are just a ways up there."

Maeve clung to him, snuggling her head tighter against his strong body. She didn't want to be left alone with Marsh even for a moment. "Take me with you," she whispered.

"Sweetheart, I have him tied tight, he isn't going to hurt you, again." He grasped her upper arms, setting her away.

She bit her lip. It was foolish to be afraid. And she hated the weakness. Zeke tipped her chin up. She looked up into his eyes. The deep brown glistened with concern and love. She swallowed the lump in her throat.

"I promise you, he can't hurt you. Sit here. I'll be back so fast you won't even know I left." His head dipped, brushing her lips with his.

A sob hiccupped when she couldn't control the emotions swirling in her chest. Tears scalded the side of her cheeks. His tenderness unraveled the last of her control. Her body shook as the fear she'd ignored while being dragged overcame her.

"Shhh, don't cry. Everything's going to be fine." He drew her into his arms, careful of her back, and held her as she sobbed. She fought to stop, but the tears and chest wracking sobs couldn't be controlled.

His strong hand held her head against his muscular chest. Licking her lips, she tasted her tears and his salty skin. She wrapped her arms around his torso, absorbing his warmth, solidness, and strength. The tears dried and she sighed—content. He was all she would ever need.

"I really should get more water." He set her away and wiped at the last of the tears dampening her face.

"I'm better now." She offered him a weak smile.

"That's the woman I love." He kissed her

briefly and stood. "Be right back."

Maeve watched him walk through the trees. He was strong, handsome, and would never leave her. Why had she been so slow to see she would never find another to love her as he did?

Movement by the horse jerked her attention to the man who wanted her dead. He'd stopped moaning and stared at her with more hatred than one person should ever harbor. I will never be safe unless this man is dead. As the thought swept through her head the man lunged, snapping the reins from the headstall on the horse and falling to the ground.

The horse reared and nickered. Marsh struggled to his feet and started toward her, hatred etched on his face and glinting in his eyes.

Maeve's heart pounded. Her gaze darted to the rifle on the ground half way between them. Could she get to it faster? She tried to push up onto her feet. Her back stung from the effort and her legs were as fragile as the soft grass under her.

She had to get to the rifle first. Swallowing the tang of fear, she crawled on her hands and knees toward the gun. The action made her back burn and sting, but she couldn't stop. Her life depended on it.

Marsh growled and shot forward.

They reached the rifle at the same time.

The glint of hatred in his eyes stalled her. Marsh lunged, knocking her over with his body. He straddled her, his knees pinning her to the ground. His weight and the wildness reflected in his eyes gave her the added strength to lash out. She dug her nails into his face, drawing blood.

"You bitch!" He awkwardly kicked her in the side of the head with his boot. Her ears rang as white lights flashed before her eyes.

Her vision cleared, and she scrambled to get away, scraping her back on the hard earth and enflaming her throbbing injuries. Desperation dispelled some of the agony, but fear held her frozen as she realized he held the rifle in his hands behind his back. He twisted his body, and the cold barrel pressed under her chin.

She wasn't ready to die, but to move with him holding the gun in such a precarious manner would surely be her death. She'd be dead when Zeke came back. No! When he came back, this monster would shoot him as well. Her mind raced trying to think of a way to save the man who had opened her heart to love.

Marsh smiled and the gun wobbled slightly.

"No!" the shout registered at the same time Zeke came into view, throwing his knife.

The gun bounced up. A shot boomed—ringing her ears and filling her nostrils with the acrid scent of burnt gunpowder. Air rushed across her face as the bullet whizzed by.

Before she could register the turn of events, Marsh tumbled forward, his eyes wide. His body sprawled over her, gasping for air, his face inches from hers.

Hysteria seized her.

She shoved out from under him, crawling backward on her hands and feet. Her lungs and throat burned from the scream searing from the pit of her belly to reach the air and emit her outrage and fear.

Maeve broke free of the man's dead weight as Zeke gathered her in his arms.

"I'm sorry. I truly didn't think he could get loose." He clutched her like a drowning man. "I would have never..."

Maeve clung to him, staring at the knife protruding from Marsh's back. And Marsh's finger poking through the trigger guard. He'd been close to killing her.

Zeke shuddered. She had to regain control. For both their sakes.

"I'm fine." She pushed, prying the tight band of his arms from across her back. She knew the fear of seeing someone you loved in danger, but his embrace also inflicted pain. A good excuse to draw away and gather her emotions.

He scanned her face and pulled back. "Damn! I forgot about your back." Guilt and shame contorted his handsome features, piercing her heart.

She held his face between her hands and waited for his dark gaze to connect with hers.

"Thank you," she said on a whoosh of pent up emotions and brushed her lips across his. She wanted to cry with happiness, but Zeke wouldn't know they were tears of joy. He'd believe he was responsible.

He placed his large, rough hands over hers, removing them from his face. "For what?"

"For coming after me, for tending my wounds, for killing Marsh, and most of all," she took a long, cleansing breath, "for loving me enough to do all of that."

Zeke growled. How long had he waited for those words to come from this woman? When he'd stepped out of the trees and saw Marsh straddling her and holding the gun on her—his body trembled at the thought of the scene he'd witnessed—he'd thought his whole world exploded with that gunshot. Now, gazing into her loving eyes and hearing the words from her soft, sweet lips—all the heartache and anguish had been worth it.

He wanted to pull her into his arms and kiss away the pain and foul memories, but Maeve's back needed tending, and they had to get to Monument in a reasonable time or Gil would round up a posse and come looking for them.

"You're welcome." He helped her to her feet, assisting her to sit on a downed log not too far from his horse. He snatched the canteen from his saddle and cut another strip from his shirt tail. Walking behind Maeve, he grimaced at the sight of the injuries reopened by her recent struggle. He should have stopped the events that marred her creamy back.

"I'll do my best not to hurt, but I can't guarantee no pain." He wet the rag and started at the top of her back.

"I understand. I'd rather face pain now than infection later."

Her bravery never ceased to amaze him. Keeping her talking might take her mind off what he had to do.

"How do you feel about staying a few days with Darcy and Gil while your back heals?" He wasn't going to broach the marriage issue until she'd had time to settle down.

"I'd rather return to teaching healed. There would be less questions." The weariness in her voice reinforced the idea. She needed rest and a chance for him to show her what life married to him would be like. And to see Halsey men didn't shackle their women when they married.

A wicked gash in the middle of her back required all his attention. He pulled out embedded slivers and small rocks, before scrubbing the dirt from the wound. She whimpered and her body trembled.

He stopped for a moment, placing his hands on her shoulders, giving her what he hoped was a comforting squeeze. "You want something to bite on while I work on this?" he asked half joking.

Her head nodded, and he looked around for a stick. He found one and handed it to her. The tears glistening in her eyes hurt like a boulder slamming him in the back. He dropped to his knees in front of her.

"You know I'd do anything to stop the pain?"

"Get to it. The faster you get it done the sooner I can stop biting this foul stick." She granted him a weak smile.

"Yes, ma'am." He moved behind her and soon had the wounds cleaned the best he could. "Okay, let's get you decent." He helped her to her feet and drew the front half of her blouse off her arms, leaving her naked from the waist up.

"You call this decent?" she asked, her eyes glittering with amusement.

"Well, I call it decent if we were in a bedroom." He cleared his throat. "Put this on." He handed her a clean shirt he'd retrieved from his saddlebag and put the one he'd cut back on. The clean shirt was large enough to not press against her back and covered her better than the tattered blouse. He helped button the shirt, allowing his knuckles to brush against her breasts. The color rose in her cheeks and heat hummed in his lower regions. Now wasn't the time to let his lust for the woman sway his intentions.

He spun her gently. The backside of her riding skirt was torn, but not through her drawers to the skin. They'd do to get her to Monument.

"You sit here and rest while I tie Marsh to his horse." She cringed and turned her back to the dead man. He didn't blame her. The hatred the man showed toward her had been deplorable.

He walked over, drew his knife out of the man's back and wiped the blade across Marsh's shoulder to clean it. Once the blade appeared clean, he sheathed the knife and dragged Marsh over to his horse. The animal snorted and side-stepped, but he managed to get the body across the saddle and secure it with the rope Marsh used on Maeve.

Tying the rope tight around the man, he felt nothing. No remorse, no anger, only justice. The man had robbed banks, killed Brendan Loman, and tried to kill Maeve. He deserved what he got.

He returned to Maeve. "Ready?"

She nodded and stood, walking to her horse. Zeke put his hands around her waist and lifted her onto the saddle.

"If you get tired, tell me. We don't have to get to Monument today." Even as he said it, he hoped they did. He wanted Maeve to spend the night in a soft, clean bed.

"I will." The look in her eyes said she wanted the same.

He mounted his horse, looped the rope from Marsh's horse around the saddle horn and headed back the way he'd come. If they kept a decent pace, they'd arrive in Monument about dark. If he was even luckier, Maeve would agree to marry him.

Chapter 22

Maeve could hardly hold her body in the saddle by the time they arrived in Monument. She'd pondered asking Zeke to stop, but the thought of a soft bed and a warm bath had kept her lips pressed together and her fatigue at bay the best she could. The sun had set after they crossed the river and headed toward town. As they passed the lit windows of the establishments, she slumped in relief.

Gil and another man stepped out of the Sheriff's office when they stopped in front of the building. "Sheriff Dore, these are the two I was headed to find." His gaze landed on Marsh. "Looks like you're doing fine."

Zeke handed the rope connected to Marsh's horse to Gil. "Take Marsh. Maeve needs a bath, a doctor, and a bed." Zeke dismounted and moved alongside her horse.

"I'll settle this and send a doctor to the hotel." Gil tugged on Marsh's horse and headed down the street.

Maeve didn't think her wobbly legs would carry her to the hotel. Before she could voice her concern, Zeke cradled her in his arms and headed toward a building with a sign proclaiming it a hotel. She looped her arms around his neck, pressing her breasts against his chest to keep pressure off her back. Her position would appear wanton to anyone watching, but the pain in her back outweighed the impropriety.

When Zeke stepped through the door, Barton rushed forward.

"Where's Marsh?" He held the door and directed them to the desk in the lobby.

"He's not a problem." Zeke stepped up to the counter. "We need a room, a bath, and when the doctor gets here, send him up to the room."

The clerk behind the desk jumped into motion at the authority ringing in Zeke's voice. "I'll have the boy bring water up immediately to room eight."

"Thanks." Zeke took the offered key. She buried her head in Zeke's shoulder unwilling to let the clerk or anyone else see her face. One thing she'd learned about herself this trip, though she'd never harbored a vain thought, she refused to let anyone other than Zeke see her at her worst.

His strong legs carried them both up a flight of stairs and down a hall. She pulled her head from the comfort of his shoulder as he leaned forward and opened a door.

The fluffy bed taking up most of the room beckoned her weary body. "The bed," she whispered as Zeke walked into the room.

"Sure you want to nestle in there before you get cleaned up?"

She pulled her gaze from the bed and stared into the concerned eyes of the man holding her. "I guess not, but can we make the bath fast?"

"I'll have you scrubbed and in that bed faster than the men around here pack water," Darcy marched into the room, if you could call a woman nearing the end of her pregnancy marching. "Zeke set her on that chair and get these lazy people around here jumpin'."

Maeve smiled at Zeke's response to his sister-in-law's orders. She found herself settled onto the only chair in the room, and Zeke headed out the door before she could even utter hello to Darcy.

The diminutive woman crossed the room and took her hand. "I'm so glad you recognized me at the bank." Her concern softened her eyes, and a genuine smile tipped the corners of her mouth.

A Chinese man, barely larger than a boy, entered with a privacy screen and retreated as Zeke carried in a large, tin tub. His gaze lingered on the tub only long enough to set it down before his brown eyes sought reassurance.

"Thank you, for bringing the tub. Darcy will help me undress while you see to the water." The glint in his eyes said the words conjured up images of her naked. Heat crept up her neck, and her cheeks flamed.

"Once you're freshened and in bed, I'll bring the doc up." He turned to Darcy. "She's got two nasty cuts on her back. Make sure they get cleaned well." He glanced at her. "You may need something to bite on again."

She didn't want to think of the pain she still had to go through. "I'll be fine, just see the water comes fast, that bed and I are going to meet real soon."

Zeke winked at her and headed back out into the hall. Darcy closed the door and dragged the screen to a corner. "Come on, let's start undressing you behind this screen."

Maeve pushed her body up out of the chair and winced as the shirt rubbed her back. "There's not much to take off of me," she muttered, stepping behind the screen as the door opened. She peeked around the end to watch the Chinese man and Zeke carry in buckets of steaming water.

The thought of soaking in the steaming water was all that kept her on her feet until Darcy dragged the chair over so she could sit while the small woman with the round belly took off her shoes.

"Should you bend over like that?" she asked, enthralled by the energy and forthright manner of the woman.

"I figure I can do anything that doesn't upset me or the baby." Darcy snorted in disgust. "I can't believe these women that hole up in their houses the last month of a pregnancy. It's a fact of life, and it sure makes Gil proud as a peacock when we walk down the street and he can show off his growing seed." Darcy laughed at her own ribald comment.

Maeve blushed and smiled. This woman was the most open and honest person she'd come across, other than Zeke.

"So Gil doesn't make you stay home. I mean, this is quite a trip you made from Galena to here and from the looks of you, you could have that child any day." Maeve stood, dropping her skirt to the floor and stepping out of it.

"The only thing Gil has made me do was promise not to touch a gun." Darcy smiled. "Which is fine with me after the trouble my shooting a bank robber caused."

The door opened, followed by the sound of pouring water, retreating steps, and the door clicking closed again.

Darcy looked around the screen. "Looks like your bath awaits." With Darcy's help, Maeve slid her arms out of the shirt Zeke gave her and then shoved her drawers to the floor.

"When I get out of the tub all I have to put back on are those dirty clothes." She glanced at the dismal pile of garments at her feet.

"I'm sure Zeke will think of that." Darcy held her arm as she stepped into the tub and lowered into the warm, inviting depths.

The water soothed her aching muscles, but she couldn't lean her back against the vessel and soak.

"Here." Darcy placed a pillow at the end by her feet. "Cross your legs and lean forward onto this."

Maeve crossed her legs and leaned against the pillow, folding her arms around the soft cushion and placing her head on it. The warm water made her legs flexible and the stretch felt good. She snuggled her face into the pillow as warm water ran down her back. This was heavenly.

"I'm afraid this is going to hurt." Darcy scrubbed on the upper part of her back. The pain brought tears to her eyes. She clenched her teeth and gripped the edge of the tub with one hand as the scrubbing moved down her back. She bit her lip to keep from crying out.

"Almost done," the waver in Darcy's voice expressed her empathy.

Warm water sluiced down her back followed by a whoosh of cool air.

"Zeke Halsey, back on out of this room!" Darcy exclaimed as the swish of her skirt faded toward the door.

"I brought clothes for Maeve and the doc's here."

Maeve buried her head on the pillow, mortified. Not only was she hunched over in a tub, but she had no idea how bad her back looked.

"I still need to wash her hair. Hold the doctor, and I'll hurry."

The door closed, and Maeve raised her head. "I'll just dress."

"No. We're going to get you all cleaned up. Hair and all. It'll make you feel better." Darcy helped her lean back in the tub and poured water over her head. "And you have a cut that needs cleaned." Small fingers scrubbed at her scalp, easing the pressure when she neared a spot on Maeve's head that was tender. It must have been where Marsh kicked her during the ordeal. Either that or when her head had smacked into rocks and sticks.

Pushing thoughts of Marsh and the past couple of days to the back of her mind, she sighed at the careful attention Darcy gave her hair. She couldn't remember the last time someone really scrubbed her hair or did something for her other than Zeke. That she was willing to be taken care of shocked her.

"Okay, you're clean." Darcy plucked a flour sack towel from the bed and Maeve stood, pulling the cloth around her.

Packages sat on the end of the bed. She moved to the bed as Darcy pulled back the covers.

"Put on some drawers and lay on your stomach." Darcy ripped open a package and handed her a new pair of lacy drawers.

Maeve smiled. Zeke liked to dress her in lace. She pulled the drawers on and crawled into bed, belly down. Darcy drew the covers up to her waist. "I'll call the doctor in."

Maeve wrapped her arms around the pillow. She didn't want to be alone with the doctor. She wanted Zeke. "Darcy?"

"Yes."

"I'd like Zeke in here, too."

Darcy watched her a moment then squeezed her shoulder. "I'll send him in." There was no censure in her voice, strengthening Maeve's resolve it was a good decision.

Muffled voices grew near, and Zeke pulled a chair up to the head of the bed. He leaned down and kissed her cheek before sitting. "Maeve, I've brought Doctor Spencer with me. He's going to fix your back."

She nodded. Her heart thudded in her chest as Zeke dug her hand out from under the pillow and held it.

Practiced hands probed her head, and then her back. She clutched Zeke's strong fingers as the doctor spread something gooey over her skin.

"You'll need to apply this ointment every day and change the bandage," a man's voice boomed above her.

"We'll be sure she's taken care of." Zeke stared down at Maeve's back. The sight wasn't as horrific as when he first washed the dirt from her, but it still tightened his gut.

He gave her fingers a reassuring squeeze and stood. He shook the doctor's hand and escorted him to the door. Darcy, who'd been standing by the door, headed to the bed.

"I can take care of things from here," she said, placing bandages on the bed beside Maeve.

"I'm not leaving until she's eaten and asleep." He closed the door and moved back across the room.

"It isn't appropriate for you to be in here." Darcy jammed her hands on her hips.

"We're chaperoned, because you're here."

Darcy tapped the toe of her shoe. "She isn't sufficiently clothed."

Zeke thought of Maeve stark naked stretched out on the chair in the shack. He grinned and waggled his eyebrows. "I know."

"Zeke Halsey, it isn't proper for you to see her..." she waved a hand over the bed, "well, to see her like this."

"I've seen her a lot worse." He knew that wasn't what his pint-size sister-in-law meant but he liked riling her.

"You..." She smacked his shoulder and har-rumphed.

"Please, Darcy, it's okay. Just get me bandaged so I can rest," Maeve said from her face down position on the bed.

"See, she doesn't mind. Let's get this done."

Zeke gently grasped Maeve's shoulders, helping her into a sitting position. He held her arms out while Darcy wrapped the bandage around her torso. When they were done, he peered into her face.

"Do you want to eat before you sleep?"

"I'm not hungry." Maeve pushed her damp, disheveled hair out of her face and peered at him. "Will you stay with me?"

"I'm not going anywhere."

She scooted to the middle of the bed and lay on her side, patting the empty space between them.

"I'm all dirty." He sat in the chair and pulled off his boots.

"I don't care."

Darcy cleared her throat. "I've a feeling I don't want to know what you two have done. I'll go see what I can scrounge up for food for when you're done sleeping."

His sister-in-law left the room. Zeke followed her and locked the door as soon as her skirt swept through the opening. He stripped off his clothes and stepped into the still full tub. The water was cooling, but it removed the worst of the dirt.

He pulled clean drawers out of the packages he'd purchased and slipped into the covers beside Maeve. She'd fallen asleep while he bathed. He lay on his side and watched her. He'd almost lost her today. When he'd found Marsh straddling Maeve and brandishing a rifle, he thought the world had come to an end. The fear that enveloped him froze him and had nearly cost Maeve her life. He never wanted to witness her in that kind of peril again. He may not be able to react as quickly the next time.

"Zeke! Zeke! Open this door!"

Zeke curled his arm around Maeve and she moaned. The pounding continued as he moved away from her back and slipped out of the bed. He pulled his trousers on and headed to the door.

"Dang, Darcy," he unlocked the door and pulled it open. Gil stood in front of his wife with his foot raised ready to kick the door in.

"What's the matter?" Zeke stepped back, allowing Gil and Darcy to enter. She carried a tray laden with food.

"Darcy has been up here twice and you haven't answered the door." Gil glanced at the bed and back at him.

"I was tired. And keep it down, Maeve's still sleeping." He tugged a clean shirt out of the open package that tumbled to the floor during his nap. As he buttoned the shirt, Darcy placed the food on a small table and moved to the bed.

"Maeve?"

"Let her sleep." He stepped between his sister-in-law and the bed.

"She needs to eat." Darcy glared up at him.

"She needs rest and food when she wakes." He crossed his arms. No one would disturb Maeve. He wanted her rested so they could discuss their future.

"Sheriff Dore needs a statement from you." Gil stood beside his wife. He, too, crossed his arms, taking a stand.

"Go with Gil," Maeve's muffled voice came

from behind him. He spun around. Maeve looked up at him. Her color was better, but the dark circles under her eyes and her pain pinched features didn't set well with him.

She motioned with a limp hand. "Go with Gil. Darcy can help me into a shift, and we can eat when you get back."

"Only if you promise you'll sleep after that." He captured her hand. He didn't want to leave her even though he knew all the threats were gone.

"I'll sleep." She gave him a weak smile. He leaned down and kissed her cheek.

Glancing at Gil, he said, "Give me a minute to get my socks and boots on."

Gil set about filling buckets from the tub and tossing the bath water out the window.

Zeke sat on the edge of the bed, wanting to stay as close to Maeve as possible. He'd come so close to losing her, he didn't want any time to slip away when they could be together. He pulled his socks on, patted her hip, and leaned down to shove a foot in his boot. A hand fluttered against his back. Warmth radiated from his heart out to his limbs. He'd worked so long to have this woman return his feelings unconditionally. To have her reach out to him now, unleashed emotions he didn't understand.

"I'll be back before you even miss me." He leaned down, brushed a wispy strand of hair off her cheek, and pressed his lips to her soft skin.

"I doubt that." Her soft whisper sent flames to his groin. He knew she was in no shape for the thoughts raging inside of him, but to know she would miss him, made the words sweeter.

"Are you coming?" Gil's irritated voice and Darcy's tapping foot were a pretty good indication the two had no idea how hard he'd fought for this bond.

He kissed Maeve's cheek one more time and stood. "Let's get this over with so I can get back."

Maeve felt his weight leave the bed. Panic squeezed her chest. She was vulnerable lying face down in the bed, it was logical she wanted the only person she trusted by her side. The door closed and the swish of skirts neared the bed.

"Are you ready to get a shift on and sit up?" Darcy's voice was not so much a question as a command.

She moaned. Her back stung, but didn't throb as it had after the bath. And she was tired of her face being smashed in the pillow and unable to see things. She pushed up into a sitting position in the middle of the bed.

"Do you want to sit at the table?" Darcy asked, holding out a clean, white shift with lace around the neckline.

Nodding, she held up her arms as Darcy dropped the garment over her head. It pooled around her before she hung her legs over the edge and stood. The world spun and whooshing noises filled her head. She plopped her bottom back on the bed and waited for the sound to abate.

"You seem to have finally come around to Zeke's way of thinking," Darcy said, handing her a glass of water.

"What do you mean?" She took a drink and watched the petite woman standing in front of her.

"He was mooning after you when I first met

him. He bestowed such virtues on you I was scared to stand next to you." She laughed and took the empty glass.

"He's been sparking me since the first time I didn't return his hello." She smiled. "He was standing on the roof of old man Gantry's barn."

Darcy laughed. "Well, you seem to be responding to his hello now."

Her face heated. She wanted all his hellos and then some. "He's kinda grown on me."

"No kidding. You two better get married soon or there's going to be talk." Darcy put her hand out to help Maeve to her feet.

Married. She accepted Darcy's help and walked to the table and chair. Would that be what Zeke would expect? She could see herself sharing blissful moments with him in the future. But was she ready to make the commitment of marriage?

Maeve pushed the hair from her face and stared out the window, avoiding the searching gaze of the woman in the opposite chair.

She wanted Zeke. He made her feel safe, secure, and happy. But did she love him enough to marry him?

Chapter 23

Zeke whistled as he checked the cinches. Maeve was ready to travel. If they left on time, they'd make Gil and Darcy's by night and arrive in Sumpter the following day. He planned to wait to ask her to marry him until she returned to teaching. After all they'd been through, if he waited until she was back in her routine, she'd know he wasn't asking her just because she'd nearly been killed. His hands fisted. He'd forever have the vision of her dangling helpless and hurt etched in his memory. He never wanted to see her in danger again.

His heart couldn't take it.

Maeve and Barton exited the hotel at the same time as Gil and Darcy approached from the street with a wagon. Zeke couldn't take his eyes off Maeve. Her coloring had improved, and he knew for a fact her back was healing. A grin tugged at his lips. He'd started the evening before checking her injuries. They'd ended with a tussle in the sheets and both of them satisfied.

"Zeke, you won't believe what Mr. Barton offered me." The enthusiasm in Maeve's voice as she hurried up to him was another sign of her healing both physically and mentally.

"What did Barton offer that has your face glowing and a pretty smile on your lips?" He stepped forward, taking her hand and drawing her in front of him. If he lived to ninety he would never get tired of gazing at her.

"He's arranged for me to go to Chicago and train to become a female Pinkerton." Her words were the equivalent of falling into a snow drift. Shock and numbness.

"Why?" he searched her radiant face. She didn't really want to put herself in danger, did she?

"I believe Miss Loman will make as good an operative as her father." Barton stepped forward, smiling like a doting parent at the woman.

Zeke searched her face. Why would she want to be in danger again? "I don't understand. You were lucky I found you. Marsh could have—" Zeke pulled her into his arms as his heart raced with dread. He couldn't go through that again.

He held her at arm's length. "Marry me. I promise you can do whatever you want, but please don't put yourself in that kind of danger."

Her eyes softened, but the determined set of her lips and ramrod back told him she would refuse. He dropped his hands.

"I'd hoped you'd come with me." Now, she grasped his hands. "We could work together." Tears glistened in her eyes. "I don't want to go back to teaching. I liked outsmarting the outlaws. Knowing

I helped put them in jail is the first thing in my life that made me feel like I made a difference."

He wanted to go with her, be with her. A Pinkerton's life would mean traveling and always staying a step ahead of the people you chased. A life of danger. A life of seeing her in danger over and over. Panic tightened his chest and pounded in his head.

"I-I can't go with you. You don't know how hard it was to see you dragged off by Marsh and know it was better to let you go than charge in and try to save you. And then, the tree..." He squeezed his eyes shut, willing the images away. His body shook. "I can't live through that. Not again." He pulled his hands from her grasped.

"But if you're there, I won't come to harm." Her voice caught on a sob.

"I was with you when Marsh..." He'd nearly gone mad with anger and fear when Marsh straddled her and held her at gun point. He couldn't live through that again and come out sane.

"Not truly, it was my fault for stopping." She clutched his shirt. "You have to come with me. I need you." Her pleading in the street with so many people as witness, nearly had him conceding. She would never show these emotions in public if she didn't feel them.

His heart ached. Damn. He wanted to go with her, love her, and protect her. Zeke squeezed his eyes shut. He couldn't watch her throw herself into danger. Not again. It hurt too damn much.

"I- can't." He pulled her into his arms and met her lips with a bruising, agonizing kiss.

Zeke leaned back and staring into Maeve's

eyes, he said to Barton, "Take care of her."

He stepped away from her and mounted his horse. Without acknowledging any of the people gawking at him, he turned his horse and raced down the street.

Maeve's heart stopped beating as the man she loved raced out of her life. She swallowed the lump of despair.

"You said you'd never leave me!" she screamed.

Strong hands grasped her shoulders. She ignored Mr. Barton and stared at the shocked faces of Gil and Darcy. "He said he'd never leave me." Anger replaced the shattering of her heart. "Just proves my point, you can't love anyone, they always leave and hurt you."

"Don't say that!" Darcy rushed toward her. "I'm sure he'll think about it and come around. It was a shock is all. He'll return."

"Mr. Barton has already telegraphed the Chicago office. They're expecting me." She faced Mr. Barton. "I'll take the train out of The Dalles. There's no sense in my going to Baker City to catch it when I'm this close to a station."

"What about your things?" Darcy asked, taking her hand. "Don't you need to go home to get your things?"

"I'll use the reward money to purchase clothes. I have nothing of importance in McEwen." Not now that Zeke abandoned me. She swung up onto the horse Zeke had prepared for their return to Sumpter.

"I'll send a telegram when I get to Chicago." She didn't want to stay another minute in this town. She looked up at the hotel that held reminders of Zeke and how close they'd become—or she thought they'd become. She'd finally found someone she believed in, and he walked out on her.

Pain ripped through her more vicious than the physical pain Marsh had inflicted on her. Her body started to double over before she stiffened her back and pulled her unemotional cloak around her sealing her off from any feelings.

"You can't ride by yourself." Barton untied Gil's horse from the back of the wagon. "I'd like to borrow this. I'll leave him in The Dalles stables."

She didn't care if the man rode with her as long as he didn't say anything. She had a lot to think about. Namely how she could have let herself be pulled in by the notion Zeke loved her enough he would never leave. First her father and now Zeke. What was wrong with her? She'd been stupid to believe all his promises. Even knowing fate had once again ripped love and happiness from her, she couldn't stop the ache gnawing at her heart.

Zeke rode as hard as his horse could go until the poor animal was exhausted. He pulled to a stop by a stream and dismounted, allowing the horse to catch its breath and drink.

Damn! Why did the woman have to be so danged independent? He wanted to hold her and love her. Grow old together, but he couldn't. Not knowing she would be in danger with each mission she went on.

His legs buckled, and he sat on a rock. Clutching his head in his hands, he searched for answers. His chest ached with loss and dread. He wanted her. Not in a lustful way, but to share his life. Being a Pinkerton there was no telling how long her life would last. It could be until they turned gray or it could end next week. He'd felt cold cocked again when she'd looked so radiant saying she wanted to be an agent.

Cutting out now was the only way to save his heart later. Maeve's words as he rode off would forever haunt him. He'd repeatedly told her he'd be there for her. He'd planned to be there for her, but... he couldn't knowing she was willing to throw away her life and their love. She'd finally believed him—and he left. He'd hurt her more than just taking away his love, he'd taken away her faith. God help him, but he was a fool.

Zeke crawled onto his horse and headed to Sumpter. To the cabin and the life he knew before meeting Maeve. He needed to get back to normal, forget her.

"What do you mean you left Maeve in Monument?" Ethan pulled him into the cabin by his shirtfront and forced him into a chair. "You talked that woman into looking for her father and you said you'd take care of her."

Zeke couldn't look at Ethan. The last day and night as he kept a steady pace toward home, he realized how much he missed Maeve and the dishonor he'd committed.

"You don't know what I went through—"

"Nothing should make you leave a woman

alone." Ethan scowled at him. "I thought I taught you better than that."

"She wasn't alone. She had Barton, Gil, and Darcy with her." But it was you she called to stay.

"After mooning over her for better than a year, why'd you all of a sudden decide she isn't what you want?" Ethan sat in the chair as Hank came in the house.

"Where's Maeve?" Hank asked, moving to the stove.

"In Monument. Alone." The words dripped with derision as Ethan stared a hole into Zeke.

"Alone? Are you an idiot?" Hank sat at the table and stared at him as well.

"You don't know the whole story." He pulled the damn tintype out of his pocket and slammed it on the table. The frame shattered, just like his heart. Ethan picked up the tintype, the backing and frame remained on the table. As he looked at the photo of their parents, Zeke noticed writing on the back. He grabbed the tintype from Ethan and flipped it over.

Brendan, if you have trouble in Oregon go to my cousin. Show him this, he'll understand.

In his mother's handwriting were his parent's names and the year they were married. William and Penelope Halsey 1855

"That's why he carried it around." Zeke dropped the tintype like a hot stick. It fluttered to the table, and guilt, stronger than he'd ever felt before, wracked him. His father's cousin had given the photo to Maeve's father knowing William would help. Maeve was Loman's daughter and he, William's son, had failed her. Failed his family.

"Damn!" He clutched his hair in his hands and hung his head. Shame slammed into him like a falling tree. He'd walked away from Maeve, from love, and all because he was scared of losing her.

The sound of a rapidly approaching horse barely registered as Zeke drowned in his guilt.

"Is Zeke back," Clay asked, entering the cabin.

"If you could call it that." Hank stood, moving away from the table.

Zeke raised his head and scanned Clay's smiling face. "Why are you looking for me?"

"Telegram came for you." He grinned. "I took the liberty of reading it to see how important it was."

Ethan grabbed the slip of paper from Clay's hand, read it, and sat it on the table in front of Zeke. "You may want to read this."

He looked at the name on the bottom. Barton. Something happened to Maeve. He snatched the paper and began reading,

In The Dalles STOP Maeve misses you STOP The Pinkerton's could use a team like you STOP We'll be in Baker City on Thursday STOP Barton STOP

"What's today?" he asked, shoving the chair back and standing.

"Wednesday." Clay picked up the telegram. "Why are you here and Maeve's in The Dalles?"

"Because our brother's an idiot," Hank chimed in.

"Yeah, I am. But I'm getting smarter." He looked around the cabin. "Boys, I need your help."

After her arrival in The Dalles, Maeve spent every waking minute preparing for her trip to Chicago and her new life. She purchased a train ticket and dresses a matron would wear. Subdued and not the least alluring. No man would look at her and think she wanted a husband. No one would break her heart, again.

She wiggled her bottom on the hard seat of the railroad car and peered out at Baker City. The conductor announced they would be held over for an undisclosed length of time and passengers should use the layover to stretch their legs. She could use a reason to get up and move around, but didn't want to set foot in Baker City. There was no one she cared to see. She wasn't ready to tell her mother what she'd found out about Pa. And Zeke would be panning for gold and have forgotten all about her, since it appeared the love he insisted he felt for her wasn't enough to keep him with her as she worked to instill justice.

Tears burned her eyes. She dabbed at them with a handkerchief and continued to stare out the window so those still moving about the car wouldn't see her vulnerability. She'd managed to keep the tears at bay during the day as she prepared for her trip. The nights, however, had been harder. She was glad Mr. Barton had readily accepted the idea of a stroll when the conductor suggested it. She was tired of his continually telling her not to give up hope. As if hope would bring Zeke back to her.

Once she arrived in Chicago and began her training, she'd be too busy to think about Zeke and the past would be just that—the past. She'd start a new life. As a Pinkerton Operative, just like her father.

Taking a deep breath, she blew her nose and stopped the tears. She'd come out of this experience stronger. No one would ever get close to her, again. Having her heart broke twice was more than enough.

"Ma'am, would you please come with me?" The conductor stood beside her seat.

She looked around. There was no one else in the car. "Why?"

"We need to clear the car." The seriousness in his voice and the way his eyes darted to the exit made her nervous.

"Is there something wrong with the railcar?"

"That's what we need to determine, ma'am." He held out a hand to help her stand.

She clutched her reticule and scanned the area outside the window. There didn't appear to be anyone she would bump into and have to explain why she hadn't been teaching and why she was on a train.

"Very well." She stood and followed the conductor to the door. At the top of the steps, she stopped. Why was a crowd gathered by the station house watching the car she exited?

"Maeve, we need to talk." The familiar voice jarred her from her thoughts. She looked down at a man dressed in a black wool suit. He held a bouquet of flowers and derby hat in one hand. The dark eyes were wary and the half smile, on lips she remembered so well, tilted in an apologetic smile.

"I'm not sure we have anything to say." Her heart rapped against her chest like a bird trying to escape. Her gloved fingers clutched her skirt as she held his gaze.

"Just hear me out, please?" He reached a hand up to her, his gaze remained locked with hers.

She wanted to take the hand, wanted to believe he was sorry for leaving. Glancing beyond him, she recognized her mother, Aunt Geraldine, the Halsey brothers, Darcy with a bundle in her arms, Darcy's brother, and Mr. Barton. Why were they all standing there grinning?

"Please, forgive me for my foolishness. I love you and have been kicking myself every day—no, every hour—that I left you at Monument." Zeke climbed the steps and offered the flowers. "I promise to never leave your side if you'll do me the honor of becoming my wife."

"Zeke...I—" She wanted to move into his arms and give him the answer he sought. But would he truly be able to keep his promise?

"What will it take to make you my wife?" The fear and love in his eyes brought a lump to her throat.

"A promise kept."

He flinched.

Her heart fluttered. He regretted his actions.

"Maeve, I'm so sorry." Zeke took her hand. "I was selfish. All I could think was to spare myself. I didn't take into consideration the ache I've had every minute since I left you." He trailed a finger down the side of her face. "Or the hurt I caused you. I broke a promise I'd made to you from the beginning of our courtship. One which you finally believed." His eyes glistened with unshed tears.

"Zeke, I—"

"Shh. Don't say anything. Think about you and me. The life we can have as Pinkerton Agents." He held her hand. The warmth and security his touch brought wrapped around her, protecting her.

She searched his eyes. "What about the mine, your family?"

"Ethan's already cooking up something to make us money without me having to be here." Zeke raised her hand to his lips. "What do you say? Will you marry me?"

"Really?" This couldn't be happening. She'd dreamed he'd find her, but upon waking had faced the truth. She held her breath.

"Yes, we're going to get married and enter the Pinkertons as husband and wife. Barton said if we're already married we'll get assignments that require two operatives."

She studied his handsome face. He meant every word. Married and joining the Pinkertons.

"That is if you'll accept my proposal." Zeke held his breath. He knew how deeply he'd hurt Maeve. It wouldn't surprise him to have her turn him down. He deserved it for the way he ran out on her. She may think him capable of doing it again.

Her head barely nodded, and a small smile raised the corners of her mouth. "I accept."

Air whooshed out of him. He swept her up into his arms. "I promise I will always be there for you as a husband and a partner."

"What made you change your mind? I mean about seeing me in danger."

He looked over at the group watching and waiting. "As much as seeing you in danger nearly killed me, I couldn't function without you. Ethan, Hank, Clay, and even Barton raked me up one side and down the other for walking out on you. And for walking out on a love a man only finds once."

"Are we ready? The train needs to leave in fifteen minutes," The conductor said, standing at the foot of the steps.

"Come on." He swept Maeve up in his arms and descended the steps.

"But the train and Chicago are that way." Maeve pointed behind them.

"But the preacher and the wedding are this way." He smiled at the surprise and delight in her eyes.

"How did you know I'd say yes?" she teased.

"I wasn't sure, but I wanted to be prepared." He placed her on her feet in front of the preacher. Their family and friends gathered behind them.

Maeve held the bouquet and recited the words Zeke had been dreaming since the day he fell for her.

"I now pronounce you husband and wife." The preacher shut his Bible and smiled at him. "You may kiss the bride."

He gathered his wife into his arms. Her shining eyes and smile fused his heart to hers.

"I love you," she whispered and placed her lips on his.

He'd longed for her to say those words. The force of their meaning reverberated to his heart. "I promise you won't ever see me walk away from you, again."

"That's good, because I won't let you."

About the Author

All my work whether it's my romance or my mysteries have Western or Native American elements in them along with hints of humor and engaging characters. My husband and I raise alfalfa hay in rural eastern Oregon. Riding horses and battling rattlesnakes, I not only write the western lifestyle, I live it.

I love to hear from fans. You can find or contact me at:
patyjag@gmail.com
or my website:
www.patyjager.net

Continue to the next page to find a listing of my historical western books or visit my website:
https://www.patyjager.net

Historical Western Romance
Gambling on an Angel
Improper Pinkerton
For a Sister's Love
Christmas Redemption

Halsey Brother Series
Marshal in Petticoats – Gil's story
Outlaw in Petticoats – Zeke's story
Miner in Petticoats – Ethan's story
Doctor in Petticoats – Clay's story
Logger in Petticoats – Hank's story

Halsey Homecoming Trilogy
Laying Claim – Jeremy's Story
Staking Claim – Colin's Story
Claiming a Heart – Donny's Story
A Husband for Christmas - Shayla's Story

Letters of Fate Trilogy
Davis
Brody
Isaac

Silver Dollar Saloon
Savannah
Lottie Mae
Freedom

Contemporary Western Romance
Perfectly Good Nanny
Bridled Heart

Historical Paranormal Romance
Spirit of the Mountain
Spirit of the Lake
Spirit of the Sky

Thank you for purchasing this Windtree Press publication.
For other books of the heart, please visit our website at
www.windtreepress.com.

For questions or more information contact us at
info@windtreepress.com.

Windtree Press
Hillsboro, OR

www.ingramcontent.com/pod-product-compliance
Lightning Source LLC
Chambersburg PA
CBHW060925190726
48286CB00002B/634